H. N.

Songs for the Sorrowing

H. N.

Songs for the Sorrowing

ISBN/EAN: 9783744772488

Printed in Europe, USA, Canada, Australia, Japan

Cover: Foto ©Andreas Hilbeck / pixelio.de

More available books at **www.hansebooks.com**

SONGS FOR THE SORROWING.

SONGS

FOR THE SORROWING.

By H. N.

WITH AN INTRODUCTION,

BY WM. R. WILLIAMS, D.D.

" Be like the bird, that halting in her flight
Awhile, on boughs too slight,
Feels them give way beneath her, and yet sings,—
Knowing that she hath wings."

VICTOR HUGO.

NEW YORK:
PHINNEY, BLAKEMAN & MASON,
BUFFALO: BREED, BUTLER, & CO.

1861.

SMITH & McDOUGAL,
STEREOTYPERS.

INTRODUCTION.

THE present volume of poems is the fragmentary memorial of one gifted and accomplished, but taken from her friends and from a widowed mother, by what, to the friends and kindred so bereaved may have seemed an untimely death. She was the only child of the late Stephen Griggs, Esq. The father, himself a man of genial temper, refined tastes, and literary culture, bestowed his best endeavors on the education of a daughter who repaid parental affection with the most attached, filial devotion. A child of early promise, her attainments were large and varied. Above all either parent felt the need of having the adornments and graces of earthly culture sustained by, and grafted upon, the great truths and controlling principles of Christ's blessed gospel. At a very early age she gave the evidence of true piety, and when between fourteen and fifteen she became a

1*

professed disciple of the Lord Jesus. During a
summer excursion, spent in part on the sea shore
of his own native Massachusetts, Mr. Griggs took
boat for a days' fishing. Although some of the
hands were experienced seamen, and in the morning there seemed little prospect of aught else than
a day of fine weather, a storm came on: and none
returned alive. The boat drifted ashore over-
turned, and after some few hours' interval, the
corpse of Mr. Griggs, wearing an expression of the
most peaceful repose, and bearing little mark of
the drifting and buffeting to which the waves had
subjected it, was also cast ashore upon another
portion of the coast. The day of the excursion
was by a melancholy coincidence the anniversary
of his wife's birth. The feelings of the wife and
child thus sorely and suddenly left alone were
those of overwhelming desolation, relieved and
chastened, however, by their entire trust in the Saviour, whose gospel the husband and father had long
and warmly loved, and in whose wise Providence
they themselves fully confided, even whilst thus
" slaying them." A glad and kind home was then
darkened. The sorrow of a daughter, remarkably

attached to her father, may be best described in the language which she used at the time in her diary from whose pages it is now transcribed :

"*November* 4th, 1850.—Well I am at home again. I have been home a long time. There is a long interval since my last entry and the present, and a longer period in my life. I have endured the greatest affliction that ever could befall me in that space of time. When last I wrote in this brief record of daily employments I was happy, I had no cares but those I made for myself, no reasonable wishes ungratified, and I was sheltered from every thing evil in the sweet, strong refuge of my father's love. Now how changed. It is the same home, the same room, nothing around me is altered, but in one fearful day all earth's hopes, peace, enjoyment, protection have left me forever. *I am fatherless.* Bitter, unwelcome truth, how gladly would I disbelieve it. The trials of past years, and they were neither few nor slight, are all swallowed up in this. We bore them patiently, cheerfully, because we had hope. Now we have none. The grave can not give up its trust; the precious clay will not revive at our bidding; the dear voice answers not our passionate invocations—we are alone. Alone, and oh how unutterably wretched. He used to think I had strength of character: I thought I had it myself, but it was the strength of the wild vine clinging to the strong trunk of its forest prop, and entwining the branches so closely with its tendrils that they could not be distinguished the one from the other. Such was my strength. He was beautiful, and noble, and powerful in his calm self-command, and I leaned upon him lovingly. When the decree went forth that he should be transplanted, if it had been done gently, and by degrees, instead of suddenly, roughly wrenching away, without a word of warning all that made life desirable, we might have borne it better. But such was not God's will. In the morning the tall tree stood without one token of decay, and bore up its feeble companions with a strong support, and at night the poor ones lay crushed and bleeding, in the mire—their prop had been cut down and carried away. But what is the use of metaphor? The horrible truth, dress it as we may, remains the same. My poor mother is a widow and I am fatherless. And the mournful remembrance that we have no last words. He may have died triumphantly; the presence of his Saviour may have so sustained him, that he may have entered with rapture into the joy of his Lord ; but we can not tell if it were so. He may have died calmly, the sober faith of a life-time not failing him at last; and this the solemnly serene countenance would seem to indicate, but we do not know that this was the way. Or as the waters cold and dark rose about his body, so the colder, darker waters of temptation may have risen on his spirit; the tempter may have buffeted him to the last, as he has since buffeted us. Agony of regret at leaving us alone in a desolate world, may have been his last thought. Worldly cares may have pressed their disturbing claims upon him; the effort to escape may have absorbed every faculty till he was exhausted. Death may have come so suddenly that all other anxieties were swallowed up in the urgent needs of his own soul, or by its slow approach may have given him time to intercede for and exhort those who died with him. All these conjectures by turns occupy us, but over all hangs the same dark uncertainty, and this increases our trial tenfold. And the last words of some Christians have been so precious to survivors as almost to take away the pain of parting. Oh my beloved father, why was I not allowed to pillow thy dying head I so fondly loved; why might I not have gone down with thee to the " swellings of Jordan." I think of that dear head tossed hither and thither by the wild waves and bruised on the rough beach, till I am wild myself. Would God I had died with thee. But he was truly mourned, and not by us only. Those who have come to sorrow with us, sorrow because they themselves lost a precious friend—somebody whom they could trust; and the one testimony from all who knew him is, that he is happy, but for us

> ' All bright hopes and hues of day
> Have faded into twilight gray.' "

After a time Miss Griggs, at the suggestion of many friends who knew the ripeness of her judgment and attainments, and who wished to see her talents employed in some such manner as would beguile her sorrow and be also useful to others, applied herself to the preparation of a Memoir, and the translation of the remains, of Jacqueline Pascal, the gifted sister of the great author of the *Provincial Letters*. The volume appeared from the press of the CARTERS in New York, and was promptly republished by NISBET in London. The *Eclectic Review*, of the latter city, spoke with warm and just praise of the freedom and racy idiomatic ease of the style, which made it difficult to regard the parts actually translated from the French as being written originally in another language than the English. But Jacqueline Pascal, although one of the first martyrs in the struggle of Jansenism against wily and relentless Jesuitism, and singularly able and earnest in defending the great truths of the gospel for which Jansenism bore its witness, was also a staunch Catholic, and the inmate of a nunnery, the famed Port Royal des Champs, whose discipline was of the strictest character.

The prevalence of the controversy provoked by the Oxford Tracts for the Times, had in Britain and America made Protestantism unwontedly jealous of all that seemed in any way to favor any

school or member of the Romish Church. Many—
not stopping to learn the real relations of the
great Jansenist body to the doctrines of grace, and
their sufferings, heroism, and genius in defense of
the vital truths of the gospel, as held in glorious
succession by Paul, Augustine, and Jansenius,
no less than by Calvin—shrunk from examining a
volume that if begun would have mastered their
sympathies, conquered their prejudices, and well
repaid their study. Though valued by those who
could judge, the book never found, therefore, the
wide currency that it merited.

As was known to her friends only, Miss Griggs
wrote in verse also on the sad calamity that had
made her home so suddenly desolate. She had
occasionally indulged and recorded her sorrow in
lines of various measure, and of unequal literary
execution. Much of real genius and some rare
felicities of expression are found in these composi-
tions. At the wish of relatives and near friends,
a few copies of these collected verses were printed
in a volume, entitled " My Father's Knell," exclu-
sively for private circulation.

The volume that now makes its appearance has

its own separate history. The health of the writer failed. The undue application in preparing for the press her Jacqueline Pascal had perhaps aided somewhat to exasperate and precipitate her sickness. She used travel and many systems of treatment, and endured great physical sufferings. in the long protracted but unavailing hope of relief from the malady that threatened to prison and cripple her. It was not the will of God that this sickness should be removed. Meanwhile, and in the periods often of keen bodily suffering, she solaced herself by the composition of poetry on various themes that presented themselves to the invalid, shut in by the walls of the sick room. But strong in Christian hope she retained, as her verses show, a true and filial grasp on the Faithful and Fatherly hand that wielded the rod of chastening, and mingled and proffered the cup of bitter but salutary affliction. Her bodily distress was such, that those who most valued her could not desire a continued stay for her on earth, amid such anguish. Favored with reason and speech to the last, she took her departure, hopefully and calmly, in the reliance on Christ's grace and faithfulness that had long blessed her, on the fourteenth day of February, 1860.

It is believed that the Christian will find much in the poetry to win and repay the attention asked for. Of more literary finish than her earlier lines, it shows glimpses of the same genius, culture, and warm affectionateness, that made her the object of true regard to her friends.

And the mother now sends forth this memorial, blessing God for such a child, and for the testimony which that child gave to the sufficiency and immutability of the gospel as a support in earth's heaviest calamities, and to its value in the anticipations it opens of that better world—where the friends in Christ now removed, may be one day rejoined—where the graces here, at best imperfect, shall be seen in their highest symmetry—and where Christ shall, by His now assembled people, be praised more worthily and be resembled more vividly and more entirely.

CONTENTS.

2*

PROEM.

ONE, of her only son bereft,
  Herself a widow, to the wave
Whose mad up-rising joyless left
  Her life, an offering gave—

Lest there, with anguish like her own,
  Might mother's heart again be wrung,
From shore to shore a bridge of stone
  With shielding rail she hung.

O'er sorrow's channel, broad and dark,
  We seek to fling no feeble span ;
There, long ago, a stately arc
  . Rose without toil of man.

No flood its piles may undermine,
  Nor furious gale the arches move ;
Upheld in peace on piers divine,
  Their keystone—" God is Love."

And they whose feet the bridge have won
  Securely, view the stream obey
That curb of power, till, fret-work done,
  It falls in sun-lit spray.

But ours too oft have strayed afar,
  And sunk in depths of gloom and mire,
While following long, for beacon-star,
  Some ray of marsh-born fire.

Now in meek penance would we plant
  Way-marks for pilgrim hearts to find,
When through morass or wood, in want
  And weariness they wind ;

With Song's clear lantern would enclose
    Some thoughts whose glow-worm light,
      in hours
Of pain, to yon sure Bridge of Woes,
    Has gently guided ours.

THE LOADSTONE FORT.

[An old Hindoo tradition tells of such a fort among the mountain ranges of India, which drew to itself the weapons of all assailants, and was, of course, impregnable.]

ARE hostile feet in hush of midnight falling
　On the hush'd snows of Himalayan hills,
Bound for the Loadstone Fort ?　No bugle's
　　calling
　Wakes inmate ere he wills.

And foes may steal unnotic'd near the trenches,
　Or with bold front in banner'd force deploy,
While each in ireful hold his falchion clenches,
　And wields with warrior's joy.

Yet from tall tower no eye of chieftain gazes
  To scan the coming of a long-fear'd harm,—
No wild alarm the sick or weary dazes ;
  Each bastion hath a charm.

And while through loadstone walls that For-
    tress draweth
  The keenest missile to its own calm side,
Vainly the war-hail flies.—No legion aweth
  Him to its Lord allied.

Scarce is a foe beheld his sword unsheathing,
  Ere sword and scabbard to the walls are flown;
Shield, helm and harness, in bright circles
    wreathing
  Like garlands, there have grown.

THOU art my Fortress, Lord ! When evils
    hound me
  In horrid chase along Life's mountain gorge,

Once in Thy Presence, harmlessly around me,
  Falls steel from Hell's red forge.

Then hold me near Thee! Through serene
    attraction
  Win Thou the arrows from my sin-pierc'd
    soul ;
And powers, long thrall'd by Self in rebel fac-
    tion,
  Within Thy force enroll !

Thus, tho' the outworks where I lean are lying
  In a low valley, near a brackish well,
The same fair banner overhead is flying
    As from the Citadel ;

And I can wait, until the clouds that trammel
  Mine upward view, melt silently away—
Till Heaven's full Sun my glorious Fort enamel
    With blazonry of Day !

SAVIOUR! HOW PEACEFULLY
THE LIFE.

SAVIOUR ! how peacefully the life,
Now with regretful murmurs rife,
  Would drop its noiseless sands,
Could we but feel each tiny grain,
Each moment fraught with joy or pain,
  Was measur'd through Thy hands.

For Thou art loving !   Thou art wise !
No fringe from Thy far-seeing eyes
  Can shut out land or sea.
Thy power, Thy love inlacing thus—
Dark though the future seem to us,
  It is not dark to Thee !

2

We do not wish Life's folded woof
Held from Thy rightful touch aloof,—
   Are glad its rule is Thine ;
Yet often faith in fear will shrink
From shape uncouth, sad hue, and think
   To change some lesser line.

A day all sunshine and soft air,
A life unshadow'd by one care,
   To our dull vision look
More suited for the hearts we prize,
As wings whereon their praise may rise ;
   Than chastening hard to brook.

But Thy calm love, Oh wiser Lord,
Thro' clouds where heaviest rain is stored,
   Can freshest verdure bring,
And bid the storms that rack our globe
Swathe in a snow-soft ermine robe
   The Royal Infant—Spring.

Then with each blackening tempest-shade,
Let Thy felt love a glory braid !
   Type of the bliss we know
Awaits Thy chosen, when at last .
True light shall stream on trials past,
   From stainless Emerald Bow !

IT CANNA BE LANG.

On a calm summer eve was the bridal
  Of one who had suffered so long,
That fond gratulation seemed idle,
  The gladness it prophesied, wrong.
She had learn'd how life's pleasures were fleeting
  As pearls which on rose-petals hang ;
And gently replied to our greeting,
          " Aweel, it canna be lang."

How sad, when young pulses are bounding
  In valleys where sweet waters well,
To hear the gay saraband rounding
  So soon, in a sorrowful knell !
Oh coffin of feasting Egyptian !
  Through garlands, through dulcimer's clang,
Still pierceth thy pallid inscription—
          " Aweel, it canna be lang !"

Yet it comes like a tender evangel,
  A love-breeze, borne over Earth's deep
In the bosom of pitying angel,
  To those who in solitude weep.
Though each morn bring thy longings denial ;
  Each twilight add pang unto pang ;
Till the final cloud fall on thy dial—
         " Aweel, it canna be lang !"

Ah ! the road whereon saint and apostle
  Once wandered, hath loiterers yet ;
Shall we murmur, if enemies jostle,
  If snares by its hedges are set ?
Shall we faint at each fresh contradiction ?
  Nay ! sing, as of old, men sang,
While flame-rings sealed fast the conviction,*
         " Aweel, it canna be lang !"

* "Be the day weary, or be the day long,
  At length it ringeth to even-song,"
was a favorite distich with the English Reformers in the
Marian persecution.

THE ANOINTED EYE.

THE fairies watched her pretty ways thoughout
    the livelong day,
And then with gifts and glozing talk they
    lured the child away ;
They lured her from the orchard-slope, a-down
    the green hill-side,
From the cottage where her mother dwelt, her
    baby-sister died.

Their carved corals clasped her arm, and Alice
    grew content
To count the spots on elfin wings, and follow
    where they went ;

To feel herself the pet and pride of all that
    laughing train,
Unweeting how her brothers wept to have her
    back again.

And guileful hands bade sleep's soft dew upon
    her eyes distil,
She slept, and wakening, lo ! her couch lay far
    within the hill ;
And daisy-chain, and cowslip-ball, at morning
    thought so fine,
Looked colorless by rainbow gems full flashing
    through the mine.

Then sang they—" Choose, fair Alice, wreath
    of jewels if you list,
" Your dark-blue eyes are lovelier than yonder
    amethyst—

"Slight value' now hath topaz ray, or ruby's
    crimson sheen,

"While we can kiss your rosy cheek, and
    claim you for our queen."

And long among those elfin hills the simple
    Alice dwelt

In pleasure, pomp, and revelry, the lapse of
    time unfelt,

Until one night the fairies said—"To-morrow,
    all alone

"Must we leave our darling mistress, on a
    mission of our own."

Though bright new toys lay round her, ere the
    troop would ride away,

It was a wistful watcher viewed their festival
    array ;

And when with . salve from casket brought
    must all their eyelids touch,
What meaning in the spell could lie, fair Alice
    wondered much.

Soon disappeared with farewell smiles the
    merry cavalcade,
While Alice felt, despite her toys and jewels,
    half afraid,
Before an hour was spent she sighed—"It
    surely must be noon ;"
When noon arrived, " How lightly now they
    dance beneath the moon."

"Where are my playmates wandering ? ah !
    did I only know,
"Doubtless I too could follow, and behold
    some rarest show."

Then on the casket fell her eye, and soon a
    shout of glee
Told her espial of the nook where gleamed its
    polished key.

One moment ere the fastening yields—another
    —and her eye
Hath met the magic ointment. With a sudden,
    sorrowing cry,
Poor Alice gazed around her on a cavern cold
    and bare
Of all save leaves and lichens grey, that imaged
    her despair.

Where gold-inwoven tapestries waved gorge-
    ously at morn,
Hung only shattered spider-webs and pensile
    moss forlorn ;

She longed, yet trembled for the sound of
    footsteps coming back,
And when they came, rich robe and plume all
    radiance seemed to lack.

Those graceful forms had hollow grown, more
    hollow still their laugh,
The luscious wine they offered her she did not
    care to quaff;
And saying, "I am weary," soon they fancied
    Alice slept,
But all the while with folded eyes, sad Alice
    lay and wept.

And long-forgotten sounds once more in
    dreamy swell uprose,
Sweet snatches of her cradle songs, prayers
    heard at Sabbath close;

She started up, the fays were gone, and in the
    distance far
A soft, faint light came struggling through
    some fissure, like a star.

Toward that far gleam then groping on with
    all her slender strength,
Behold it waxing broader, ever broader, till at
    length
Deep down within the opening a flood of glory
    rolled—
And the Summer was before her in its garb of
    green and gold.

Fast paled her elfin livery before that vision
    rare—
And when could elfin lullaby with voice of
    home compare?

Safe in her old meek place of rest, she dwells
    by mother's knee :
None Alice thence shall ever wile with fraud-
    ful gem or plea.

O Lord ! if thine anointing Love have shown
    our souls how bare
Of truest joy are Earth's delights, her pa-
    geantry and glare—
If from Thy holy heaven of Light a single
    guiding ray
Through ice-rift of the glacier—Self—have
    forced its reinless way.

Still may Thy mercy lead us on, still with
    Thy strength infuse
The feeble faith that else would sink at mo-
    mentary bruise—

Till, dwelling in Thy Sun-light, joyous angel-
    welcomes ring
To hail us safe and satisfied, before Thee, O
    our King !

TIRED HEART, SLEEP.

TIRED Heart, sleep !
Sleep on quiet pillow !
Though around thee leap
Foam of wind-lashed billow,
Safe as in calm nook,
Which fair Summer ruleth,
Sleep ! thy Saviour's look
Cloud and rough wind schooleth.

Tired Heart, sleep !
Tired of wistful grieving—
Grieve no more, nor keep
Watch o'er waves thou 'rt leaving !
Let tho night-glooms rise,
Dark as wing of raven,

For thy pinnace flies
  Fast toward blissful haven.

Tired Heart, sleep !
All Earth's woe is wafted
  Soon away, while deep
Are thy joys engrafted
In a Saviour's cross—
  Starred with light unwaning !
Root, whence pain and loss
  Win immortal gaining !

Tired Heart, sleep !
Till thy Lord's hand, closing
  Eyes long prone to weep,
End, too, thy reposing :
Then awake and sing !
  Where Life's glorious river—
Fed from love's full spring—
  Tires no more for ever !

LITTLE CARRIE.

A MOTHER'S TALE.

———◆———

SNOW-DRIFTS like sentinels were filed
Against the chamber where my child
Slept in the hush they made, and smiled.

My Carrie! fair as wreath of snow—
Her cheeks with sunrise flush aglow—
Her hair like sunset's amber flow.

Ah! well I know that love is kind,
And will, in homeliest features find
Charms to which common eyes are blind:

3*

But ever, where my Carrie went,
Looks on her loveliness were bent,
Which said, " Beware ! the child is lent :

" Nay, clasp her not with such delight,
For angels' hold on earth is slight,
And she will seek the land of light !"

Some infant smiles like sunbeams stray ;
Hers in our dwelling old and gray,
Shone more like moonlight's mellow ray.

For thoughtful seemed her eyes' deep blue,
As though their mute child-wisdom knew
Of much beyond our mortal view ;

Yet soon again some baby-wile,
Or dimpling of her roguish smile,
Would fondest mother-fears beguile.

Thus eighteen months had slipped away,
When Carrie climbed, one summer day,
To ivory keys, and feigned to play.

The waxen fingers woke faint clang;
But like a lark's her clear voice rang—
I stopped and marvelled while she sang;

Then left her on some brief employ—
Sweet croon of welcome! with what joy
It told my absence gave annoy.

That night she sickened. Short the space,
I held her in my sad embrace,
Watching the languors on her face,

Before a change came o'er her mien;
Her look grew saint-like and serene,
Toward bitter cup turned gentle e'en—

Small finger pointed—pale lips tried
To drink in vain—and to my side
More closely nestling, Carrie died.

That voice of music filled mine ears,
I clasped her close in dreams for years,
At day-dawn missed her, blind with tears :

But now those faithless tears are dried ;
Here at my calling could she glide,
I would not call her to my side.

From vision of her Saviour-King,
From blisses past imagining,
Dare love like mine its dear one bring

Where sin might soil my snow-wreath fair—
Her clear voice moan in Earth's despair ?—
Ah no !   I would we all were there !

THE ORANGE-TREE.

"Le Fruit ne fait pas tomber la fleur."

No work of grace will ripen, some have said,
    With bloom unshed ;
All fair young petals lose, in Summer's glow,
    Their spotless snow ;
And holy fervors thus through trial thin
    Ere fruits begin.

But make my life, O Lord, an orange-tree,
    Thick hung for thee,
With golden deeds of mercy by whose side
    Meek prayers abide ;
Thus yielding to Thy glory, every hour,
    Love's fruit and flower.

COLIGNI AND L'ESTRANGE.

AN INCIDENT IN THE WARS OF THE REFORMATION.

BORNE away from battle surges
   Where white crests of kinsfolk meet—
While around despairing dirges
   Moan for Moncontour's defeat,
Throbs the heart at sunrise eager
   France with brave right arms to free
From proud hoof of Priest and Leaguer,
   Spurred and reined by Holy See :
And while sunset slowly dies,
That dear hope in death-shroud lies
Stark before his wearied eyes.

Through the day when steel clashed madly
  Was Coligni's helmet seen,
If the van-guard wavered, gladly
  Pressing where their place had been :
Now a closely-curtained litter
  Veils from all the warrior's frame,
Smart of wounds, though keen, less bitter
  Than his sense of grief and shame,
Heaping fast on burning brain,
  Fuel, memories of pain,
  Prayers and toilings spent in vain.

Foes who long his Faith have slandered ;
  Comrades recreant to their God ;
Worse, far worse, the Holy Standard
  Now by heel of scoffers trod ;
Each sad thought through wan cheek tingling
  With a sudden fever-glow,
Till the poisoned waves commingling
  Bid Faith's chalice overflow—

Thus while powers of darkness reign
Better had the brave heart lain
Cold among yon piles of slain !

And perchance the soul reflective
  In that hour of gloom might peer
Onward till in dim perspective
  It discerned a darker year,
When with band of butchers gory
  Guise at dead of night uprose—
When Coligni's head, grown hoary,
  Bowed beneath assassin's blows—
Royal feastings, bridal ring,
Naught but snares of hell to bring
Birds to slaughter, else a-wing.

Twilight fell o'er wold and meadow—
  Dawn upheld her shield of flame—
Only dreams of heavier shadow
  Round the imprisoned warrior came,

Till a hand its veil unfolding,
  Tramp of spearmen toward his cell
Bore another litter holding
  Frame and spirit pained as well ;
Yet he welcomed not his friend,
Comfort there was none to lend ;
Coward plainings served no end.

Soon L'Estrange's sight grew dimmer
  Watching the belovéd brow ;
Fain would Love with moonlight shimmer
  That grief-furrowed lake endow.
" Yet is God sweet consolation"
  Fell at length from quivering lip ;
Then he turned in agitation
  Stifling sobs that else would slip
Strongest leash of manly pride,
Bound all agonies to hide
From the soldiers ranged beside.

Long, with face in pillow buried,
    Long and slowly wept L'Estrange,
Weeping, while his whisper hurried
    Brought Coligni blissful change.
Swift as breath of summer sounding
    Thrills through gloomiest grove of pine—
Joyful thoughts, of God's abounding
    Strength and succour, sped like wine
Through the wounded leader's veins ;
Taught him tears and toil and pains,
Harm not whom the Lord sustains.

Voice of holiest pastor never
    (Said he oft in after-days)
Could his soul to brave endeavor
    Stir like those fond words and gaze.
Sown in tears, the flower sprang faster,
    Though by sower soon forgot,
Blooming long, an autumn aster,
    Whose mild beauty altered not

Till that fateful midnight frown,
When a mangled corpse fell down,
And the Martyr won his crown ! .

ANYTHING BUT THIS.

"Some other sorrow! Lord," I cried,
"Thine arsenal of woe is wide;
   Lift from its gleaming rows
  Some blunter weapon! Pain, disease,
  And death are powerless till Thou please—
   All grief Thine impress knows.

"Well may my spirit faint with fear:
  This blessing lost—and earth lies drear:
   Take not my only joy!
  Think on past years of mournful pain;
  Oh let Thy love, with genial rain,
   Revive, and not destroy!"

From cloud-pavilions answer came :
"Shall sinful man his Saviour blame ?
     Wilt thou, O vine so frail !
Choose where the knife shall prune away
Tendrils that on thy life-sap prey,
     And make thy clusters fail ?

" The closeness of thy twining grasp
Proves but the need of surly rasp,
     Of wrenching swift and strong,
To move away that precious thing,
The trellis where thy love-shoots cling :
     Nor can the doom be wrong.

" This is thine idol. Fearful heart,
Christ reigns alone. If His thou art,
     Know, He will surely trim
Each vagrant love away, yet give
Strength by His own true word to live—·
     To lean on none but Him !"

5*

DISTANCE REMOVED.—DARKNESS REMOVED.

St. John, xvii. v. 24.

———◆———

THROUGH ages hearts have stirr'd
  With changeful thoughts of Heaven,—
With woof of sign and gorgeous word,
  To enweave its splendors striven.

As when from altar-panes
  One light, in parting prism
Of vermeil green, and violet stains,
  Streams down on royal chrism ;

Each varying hue of bliss
  Through the mind's oriel thrown,
Seems but a pencil, born of this,
  "All gloom—all distance gone !"

Let aliens dream how bright,
   Were thoroughfares of gold—
The saint's eye craves alone for light,
   Thy glory to behold.

And where, O Christ ! Thou art,
   Thy chosen long to be :
That far land draws the faithful heart
   With but one Magnet—Thee !

THE FEAR OF EVIL.

"Quiet from fear of evil"—PROV. i. 33.

"Afraid, because of the sword of the angel of the Lord."
1 CHRON. xxi. 30.

CRUSHED as by cairn of sorrows, Lord, I lie ;
  Nor would I murmur at Thy faultless will,
But sad thoughts lodge within me, and they fly
  Aloft like chaff, though I would hold them
    still.
      Ah ! were they golden wheat,
      Thy winnowing fan to meet,
In trustful quiet, need I fear no ill.

The fear of evil ! 'Tis an evil thing—
  For in Thy presence, that all-shadowing
    Tree—

The heart should build her nest, and, bird-like,
    sing,
  Leaving the morrow's care, a charge for
    Thee ;
      Not quail, as lonely hare
      Sinks down, in sombre lair,
  Hearing far bugles, though the woods are free.

He who on couch of anguish long hath lain,
  Winces in presage of the coming blast,
And feels in every pulse some herald-pain,
  Ere yet one cloud the blue air overcast.
      My soul, too, quick of nerve,
      Will even in sunshine swerve
When change impendeth, shrinking back
  aghast.

Often, if grief hath come, I tremble less,
  Worse the foreboding than the woe, when
    here,

And ere it passes, oft with half-caress,
  I would detain it, lest some other fear,
      Through yet undarkened place,
      View, in funereal pace,
  New mourners come and go, like Highland
    seer.

So, in old pictures have I marked the fiend
  Lifting from coil of gloom a look askance
Toward bright archangel who above him leaned,
    And brandished near his brow puissant
    lance,
      As though the dusky shape
      Sought vainly to escape
  Keen blade of vengeance, and far keener
  glance.

Ah ! give me, Lord, a willingness to be
  Made through much suffering to thy. saints
  akin,

Give faith above all menaced blows to see
   Hands of Thine angels wield the javelin,
     To know, when sorrow near
      Hangs poised, with flashing spear,
What writhes within me is the Demon—Sin !

HERE AND HEREAFTER.

My life is a sluggish river,
   Winding its dull career
Through flats whereon north winds shiver,
   In the desolate region—HERE.

Once it flashed forth like a torrent,
   Lavish of diamond spray—
Passed where dark boulders horrent
   Shielded its sinuous way—

And thence through an outlet of Sorrow,
   In stupor and silence it came
Where To-day is the type of To-morrow,
   And all its gay flashes are tame.

Far down in the channel are steeping
   Ashes of hopes long dead,
As the wild Goth warrior sleeping
   In his slave-river's bed.

Faintly heaven's sunlight above me
   Falls on miasma of fears,—
Friends who most tenderly love me
   Give me small solace save tears.

But from the fair realms—HEREAFTER,
   Sorrow and sighing flee !
Sobs are unechoed by rafter
   Of dwellings through grace made free !

None grieve o'er a love too shallow
   To quiet the soul's deep thirst—
For the fullness of God will hallow
   Their bliss, who have loved Him first.

None pause by a sweet rose-thicket,
  Whose pathways green mosses pave ;
To weep because close-barred wicket
  Defends it, or worse—a grave.

None grieve over a long-sought treasure
  Through seeking, sullied and torn ;
For the lilies of sinless pleasure
  Grow not in hedges of thorn.

Fade then, ye love-lights ! spangling
  Time with your peaceful ray ;
Break, fond earth-meshes ! entangling
  Hearts from their heavenward way.

Seems cry of the night-owl dreary ?
  Dawn cometh to lift the cloud,
Then for watchers no longer weary
  Will song of the lark be loud.

Of the lark !—To the soul far sweeter
Than ever morn-music rose,
Shall the welcome of Jesus greet her,
Escaping from Sin's last woes.

THE OPAL RING.

An opal's fire-in-snow
   Gleams on a young girl's hand,
While gentle whispers show
   A charm in the golden band.

Not alone that a faëry spell
   Will shiver the radiant stone,
When its fading sparkles tell
   Of a fond love faithless grown.

For words in the gift are shrined
   From a royal Psalmist's scroll,
And the jeweled ring is lined
   With a jewel for her soul.

Awhile the maiden kept
　That charm unbroken—Then
O'er the shattered opal wept,
　And the shattered faith of men.

Gone were the glow and sheen
　Of giver and of gem—
But the golden light serene
　Of the psalm—went not with them.

IN SIGHT OF HEAVEN.

A Pioneer Missionary, who was found frozen to death on the bank of one of the Western Rivers which he had just succeeded in crossing, held in his hand a paper, and on it were feebly penciled the words "in sight of heaven."

O TRIUMPH-glance of Pilot, first in view of
    broad New World !
O Flag, by weak hands waved aloft, and held
    in death unfurled !
Pale blossoms are ye, born of Earth, to die by
    March-winds driven,
Beside this autumn-fruit of Faith, that glows
    " in sight of heaven."

Yet Earth has had her conquerors, and prince
    and peasant name
Entwine in gorgeous blazonry along the scroll
    of Fame,

And glorious memories are embalmed among
    her priceless things—
Of warriors brave and rulers wise, true poets,
    patriot-kings.

But this man more than conqueror through
    might of love became,
To bear through frontier-wilds the Cross with
    loyal hand his aim;
And never yet hath minstrel heart, by love or
    sorrow riven,
Indited loftier line than this last shout "in
    sight of heaven."

Not over pleasant garden-paths, or prairies
    green and gay
With turf and flowers upspringing fast, God's
    herald took his way;

Nor was he cheered by kindly voice, compan-
   ionship and smile,
Sent forth to thread the wilderness where silent
   Indians file.

He lay not on a peaceful couch, within a quiet
   room,
While friends and kindred paved with love his
   passage to the tomb;   .
No brother came to bid him place his confi-
   dence on high;
No worldling gazed with awe-filled mien "to
   see a Christian die."

But in the gloom of forest-ways by fleet hoof
   seldom trod
The lone man faced his foe, alone, and sank on
   stranger-sod: .

He had forded one wide river, it was dark,
    and deep, and cold ;
Another and a mightier across his pathway
    . rolled.

Alone ? ah no ! for angel-friends around him
    came and stood
To watch that calm death-duel fought beneath
    the leafless wood ;
To see those stiffening fingers their triumphant
    record trace
And the martyr-light of gladness pierce
    through pallor of his face.

Alone ? ah no ! in closer grasp than mother's
    fondest hold,
The Lord of Life and Death received that soul
    to bliss untold.

There was no need of human help when Christ
    could ease the chill,
And gently touch the throbbing breast, and
    bid the pulse be still.

Bright is the sunset splendor thrown from
    many a dying bed,
And eloquent the influence of all the saintly
    dead—
Far down the turbid waves of Time those rays
    will burn and beam,
As lighted pinnace launched by night on
    Oriental stream.

Sea-curtains veil the sleep of some, and graves
    on heathen strand
Will hear as soon the trump of God as graves
    in Father-land.

Yet dwell the parting words of none more
sweetly on mine ear
Than the death-sign made in silence by this
lonely Pioneer.

And thus, oh slothful heart of mine ! if thou
wert also found
Dauntless in labor for thy Lord, though drear-
ness abound—
Linked to His heart with bands of love, by
death or life unriven,
Thou too wouldst wait for dying grace, and
live "in sight of heaven."

THE BUILDING OF THE TEMPLE.

1 Kings, chap. vi., v. 7.

Silence ! the Fane of Jehovah is rising,
   Calm in its splendor, each stone like a gem :
Silence ! no hammer may fall, advertising
   All the long labor on Earth's Diadem.

Softly, yet swiftly, unmarred by one hap-stone,
   Springs the tall fabric, till cedar and gold
Wind o'er its surface from corner to cap-stone,
   Mirror the sunlight in every fair fold.

Walls ! in your glory and fragrance so gentle,
   Skill of slave-Afreet, through amulet sought

Doubtless in sea-cave, hath carved you as rental,
 Winning brief freedom, for Solomon wrought.

Nay. By long patience the marbles were quar-
  ried,
 Each with a mallet no veinings might foil ;
Stroke fell on stroke, to their home until car-
  ried,
 Perfect at last through the magic of Toil.

Thus while our King this true Temple is rear-
  ing,
 Silence enshrouds it. In chambers apart
Sorrow and Pain with keen chisel are clearing
 Each for fit lodgment some desolate heart.

What if that heart, full of grief and self-loath-
  ing,
 Lie 'neath their shaping in darkness and
  dread,

Gladness awaiteth it ; cedary clothing,
  Glimmer of gold shall its form overspread.

Yea, though we see not the glory now working,
  Soon shall God's temple shine forth in its
      strength ;
Shrink not from touch of the chisel, lest shirk-
      ing
  Pain, thou lose also the brightness at length.

IF ALL ALONG OUR EARTHLY WAY.

If all along our earthly way,
  No warmth or brightness fell,
But Grief kept with us day by day,
  From morn to midnight bell—
And yet at last the dawning light
Of Heaven's full splendor fringed Earth's
      night,—
Who could say aught of cross or blight
  Save—" All was ordered well ?"

But now, though every mournful year
  Seem strewn with loss and pain,
As woodland walk when leaves lie sere,
  Yet hath it herbs of gain—

Like evergreens to front the gale·
Rise Faith and Hope, and on the trail
Red foot-prints of our Lord we hail—
    Each mile makes less remain.

No needless grief lies in His plan—
    No wanton prick of thorn ;
He was on earth a sorrowing Man,
    By toil and travel worn.
Up ! laggard heart—and praises lift—
True good from seeming evil sift ;
Life hath no storm, nor blinding drift,
    But with Him may be borne !

BURIED IN JERUSALEM.

The only son of a wealthy Catholic family, left motherless while an infant, was educated, together with a sister but one year older, in rigid adherence to the Roman faith. Yet even in early childhood, he refused to repeat the Paternosters often enjoined as a penance, and would ask, "What is the use of my saying those words over when I don't want to? God will not hear me, I'm sure. It is not prayer, unless I really want to pray." And rather than yield, he would patiently bear solitude, with bread and water.

When about twelve he was placed in a Jesuit school, more than two hundred miles distant from his home. Quickly disgusted with its customs, he contrived, with equal ingenuity and daring, to escape, and made his way afoot to his father, who, although desirous for these children to be trained into good Catholics, was himself but a lax one. Remonstrance from him, threats from other relatives, and the cajolery of his frightened teachers, were alike vain. Go back the boy would not. "If you insist on my going, papa," said he, "I shall have to run away again; only instead of coming to you, I must go to some place where no Jesuit can hunt me out, and you will never see me again. They talk smoothly enough to you, and promise fairly; but if you knew as much as I do about their deceitful ways, you would sooner kill me than let one of them come near me." The father wisely yielded. The son grew up under happier influences—a young man of great promise, and of most winning disposition. Just as he had, with a tutor, made the tour of Europe, and was expected home, where every preparation to celebrate his coming of age had been completed, he died in the Holy Land, of fever, and was buried in Jerusalem. The shock to his sister was so severe, that she went at once into a convent.

Home rejoicings all are ready,
Planned for welcome of the heir,

(And hilarious voices eddy
　　Through the cool soft English air,)
　　　　Home from Tyrian
　　　　Sands, and Syrian
Fatal noon-shafts smiting now
On his broad, ingenuous brow.

How will joy the brown cheek dimple,
　　Gladness flash from bright blue eyes,
While for Eastern veil and wimple,
　　Smile of sister he descries'!
　　　　When hath newer
　　　　Love been truer
Than the sister's and the brother's
Who have never known a mother's ?

Ah ! while her fond eyes are holding
　　Lengthened vigils to devise
Warmth of welcome, his are folding
　　Calmly, 'neath Judean skies :

There they laid him—
None could aid him—
None the cruel death-wave stem :
Burying in Jerusalem.

And the sunlight is as pleasant
On sea-path of hurrying keel,
As the wish of guest and peasant
Would on festal morning feel ;
News for wailing
Unavailing
Though her swift sails waft to them,
" Buried in Jerusalem."

And they weep,—but woe far deeper
Dashes with each gasping breath
O'er her soul, who for the sleeper
Watch'd with love more strong than death.
Doubt assails her,
Faith nigh fails her,

Maddening fears his future hem—
" Buried in Jerusalem."

Large her love, her judgment weakly,
   While the priesthood's will was strong ;
And she bowed o'er missal meekly,
   Trained in self-negation long ;
      Heavenward sending
      Prayers unending
   For her heart's one priceless gem,
" Buried in Jerusalem."

Are we sure his youthful lightness
   Cared not for a Saviour's love ?
Must Earth's bloom keep out the brightness
   Of Jerusalem above ?
      Mirth's sweet laughing
      Mar the engraffing
   Of Heaven's fruit on that frail stem,
" Buried in Jerusalem ?"

Truthful lips that would not mutter
  For a penance, unfelt prayer,
Learned they not the truths which flutter
  Even yet in Syrian air ?
        Did he wander
        There, nor ponder
  On the Plant of Bethlehem
  " Buried in Jerusalem ?"

Could that fiery heart, escaping·
  Early from the Jesuit's rein,
Loathing every lie-fraught aping
  Of God's service, sought for gain—
        So have dwindled
        That it kindled
  Naught, save embers of dull phlegm,
  Gazing on Jerusalem ?

Nay ! the Holy Land is haunted
  Still by presence of the Lord ;

Birds through whom He taught have chanted
  His pure lessons while they soared ;
    Palmers dying
    Traced their flying—
  Worshipped One who rose, like them,
  Sky-ward from Jerusalem. .

Thus, in loving Hands we leave him,
  Hands that—wiser far than we—
Longed a deathless crown to weave him,
  And from death-nails would not flee :
    Hands whose Mightful
    Rule is rightful—
  His, who came not to condemn !—
  " Buried in Jerusalem."

"ROSE-WATER SURGERY."

"Great furnace for great faith." So spake my
friends,
When surging flames of trial round me
rose :
" God hath especial jewels, and on those
"He would make brightest, longest toil ex-
pends"—
And, " Sorrow's filing clearer luster lends
" To the true diamond ; with each rasping
grows
"Her power of flashing back prismatic
glows"—
Ah loving words ! which soul more loving sends

To cheer the mourner.   But my spirit sank
Within me while I heard them. Conscience
    knew
  My patient smiling veiled a will that
    shrank
In vain impatience from the cup I drank.
Yon high consolings suit a saintly few
Made meet for Heaven.   Of me they are not
    true !

PROBING.

Much had I pondered o'er the intricate way
    Whereby I travelled, deeming one so weak
    More needed velvet sward and runnels meek
Than crag and torrent, till I chanced one day
On a wise man's experience, wont to say
    " Not always do deep battle-scars bespeak
    " The warriors who for Heaven's high
        laurels seek ;
" Often in forefront of the hottest fray
    " God sets His greatest cowards, whence
        to fly
    " Were hopeless ruin—they must fight or
        die !"

8

Rough yet true teaching—proven to my cost.
  I feel the war-waves dash—my death-doom
        nigh.
Oh Lord and Marshal of thy martyr-host,
Nerve Thou my recreant soul, or I am lost !

TO A SPIRITUALIST.

O FRIEND ! Our Father doubtless hath fair
    gardens
  Beyond the walls we see ;
With restful glades, and souls we love for
    wardens,
  But—HE hath kept the key.

And yet hath told us, star-bright angels hover
  (Though with unvoiced name)*
Around our ways, and our weak warfare cover
  With shield and sword of flame.

* Judges xiii. 18.

Thus when our changeful time another teach-
    ing
  Would through old charms enthral
'Neath a new tree of knowledge, widely reach-
    ing
  With fruit and songs for all ;—

That rosy rind for me hides core of ashes :
  The song-notes I have heard
Stir not my soul, as when true heart-fire flashes
  Forth from the Master's Word.

Fain—till His love the flow of anguish stanches,
  When our belovéd flee,
Fain would we follow where each frail raft
    launches
  Far on the Eternal Sea !

Fain would we hear their new-found joy out-
    gushing
    In Heaven's triumphant psalms,
And feel a fragrance round our foreheads
    rushing
    Fann'd from their deathless palms !

Yet,—by the Way of Life, erewhile so narrow
    Lies there this sunken fence ?
Falls the Bright Shaft of God an aimless arrow,
    Foiled by our finer sense ?

Need we no more the Immortal intercession,
    The Sinless life-drops shed ?
Led on through spheres of light in far pro-
    gression,
    By spirits of our Dead—

8*

Our ransomed Dead, who clasped the Cross in
    dying
    With else despairing clutch ;
And felt a Strong Right Arm beneath them
    lying,
    His—whom they loved so much—

The long, long line of souls who have not
    faltered
    From rack or fiery crown,
But held in love the One True Faith unaltered,
    Let Queen or Kaiser frown.

Have *all* returned, the cheerless rumor bringing
    That clasp and faith were vain ?
With a wild dissonance of voices singing
    Each some untuneful strain ?

Nay—the old Spring by Beth-le-hem's Gate
    up-welling
  Thought's vexing fever cools
More than a haze of myriad rain-drops swelling
    What may be mirage-pools.

And though Our Father doubtless hath fair
    gardens
  Beyond the walls we see ;
Till in good pleasure He unvail their wardens,
    We will not crave the key.

AN INCIDENT.

"GRIEVE not, love," a mother said,
"If some morning, in my bed
   Gazing, thou should'st find me dead.

"Grieve not, daughter, if at night
   Dons my soul her robe of light—
   Through Redeeming love made white;

"Mine this plea of boding fear,
   Urged through many a prayerful year,
   'While I sleep, may Death draw near!'

"Not because 'twere sad to go
   From thy side, best-loved below!—
   Whom I have believed, I know;

" And His love, through love's sweet law,
 Since its rich depths first I saw,
 All my love hath power to draw.

" But should lingering Death unlink
 Slowly all Earth's chains, I think
 Flesh must quiver—Faith must sink.

" Doubtless, He who knows my frame,
 In night-watches oft who came,
 Will in east-wind rough-wind tame,—

" Seal mine eyes from deathly cares—
 Place me—granting life-long prayers—
 Among angels unawares."

 Thus the dreamer. Ah ! not so
 Would her Lord His glory show,
 Blindfold home she might not go.

Not in slumber's silence bound,
Hath her prayer its guerdon found,—
Is the unconscious victor crowned.

Through long months of lingering pain,
Pangs of body, heart and brain,
Sadly, slowly, life must wane.

Lava-like, the death-blow crept
O'er Hope's vineyard, yet she kept
Patient watch the while, nor wept.

One who drinks delicious wine
From the press of fruits divine,
Grapes of earth may well resign.

Arms whose strength tried wrestler knows
Mighty against myriad foes,
'Neath that timorous heart uprose:

In the last hour, feared so long,
Faith, thus held, grew eagle-strong,
And her soul passed home in song.

"APPEAR NOT UNTO MEN TO FAST."

MATT., chap. vi., v. 18.

———◆———

Not alone from food when fasting,
   Shun the look of proud Essene ;
Famine of the soul, more lasting,
   Vail thou, too, 'neath smiles serene,
Mutely, when thy sorrows darken,
   Keep them for a Saviour's eye,
Nor in haunts where man may hearken,
   Loosen from thy heart one cry.

How may friends with woe unladed,
   Lift thy burthen, soothe thy moan ?
Let not Christ's love seem upbraided
   Through keen plaints of souls, His own !

Would'st thou still the ceaseless craving
  For some dear voice, silent now ?
Think ! the grief whose sharp engraving
  Seams thy forehead, marked His brow !

Well He notes each keen incision
  Views thy heart-stripes, roughly scored,
And reserves the open vision
  Of His love for thy reward !
Soon, from rock of memories bitter,
  At His Word will fountains burst ;
And their rills by sand-paths glitter,
  Quenching even long love-thirst.

Is thy fast in lonelier fashion
  Kept beneath a leaden cloud,
'Twixt thy prayers and His compassion,
  Drifting, with wierd face endowed ?
Tell not loss of light so treasured
  To the world in loud lament ;

Lest it scoff—"Thy God hath measured
   Cup that yields not my content."

Gem of cost He counts the pleading
   Sacred to His ear alone—
While His loving Prescience, reading
   How thy faith subdues each groan—
With dark thoughts declines to palter,—
   Leaves His ordering unarraigned—
Will, at length, mute patience alter
   Into smiles of peace unfeigned.

OCEAN BLOSSOMS.

Sent with a volume of pressed seaweeds to a Missionary kinsman in Burmah.

Roses and lilies are fair to view,
   But roses and lilies fade—
The daffodil loses her golden hue,
   The violet wilts in the shade,
And the hare-bell revels in light and dew,
   On the heath where her clan have decayed.

Dimmer of outline, and duller far
   Though the fragile sea-flowers be,
Though tangles and gravel their beauty mar
   And they float where so few may see
How the Deep hath mosses that delicate are
   As the daintiest growth of the lea ;

Yet they crave but a cleansing from meaner things,
    Ere the fairy-like waifs unfold
In a thousand fibres and flexile rings,
    Crimson, and brown, and gold ;
While each to the leaf's white surface clings
    With an unrelaxing hold.

So hast thou seen on the heathen shore,
    Many a spirit lie,
Darkened with evil encrusting o'er
    Hopes of as rich a dye,
As thine own eyes view when they meekly pore
    O'er the promise of life on high.

So, too, from sands of its native lair,
    Lifted with loving hand,
Patiently tended in faith and prayer,
    Shall the human flower expand,
Till it rivals in tissue and coloring rare
    The bloom of a happier land.

And it will not wither.   The rose we spoil
  When her stem from the root we sever;
But the *souls* thou art winning through tears
    and toil,
  By decaying grieve thee never:
In the Book of Life they are safe from soil,
  And their loveliness lasts for ever.

9*

SABBATHS AT HOME.

GLAD bells announce the coming
　　Of a holy Sabbath-time,
Yet bring the thought benumbing
　　For me they do not chime.
Ah ! not for me the blessing
　　In God's own Temple heard,
By lowly hearts confessing
　　How widely they have erred.

Ye fleece-clouds floating o'er us !
　　Above you songs ascend
In earth's encircling chorus,
　　To Earth's One Glorious Friend.

Youth in His Love rejoices,
   While children lisp the praise
That swells from manly voices,
   And ancients full of days.

Yet grieve we for the scoffers,
   Who scorn Him and deride—
Or from His loving proffers
   For world-lures turn aside.
For tares shall wheat encumber,
   Till the Millennial Song
From lips no tongue may number,
   Rise and reverberate long.

O ! lovely, lovely vision
   Of the Redeemer's reign !
Swaying to meek submission
   Each heart as well as fane—

Bidding a rainbow glisten
　　Through every gathering tear,
While for our Lord we listen,
　　And deem His Chariot near.

What if the weary chastening
　　Which holds us far away
From service, should be hastening
　　That pledged Possession-Day !
The faith and patience proven
　　In many a lonely room,
Be silver threads inwoven
　　With glory in His Loom !

And painful though our severance
　　From Zion's holy Hill,
Yet bowing low in reverence
　　Before the righteous Will.

A sense of Christ's dear Presence
   May on the desert bare
Fall, with diviner essence
   Than erst in place of prayer.

Yea! if the Dismal Valley
   To dreary prescience ope,
One thought anew should rally
   Our half-exhausted hope,
And gleam as dove-wings given
   To lift some grovelling gnome—
" *Our Sabbath-hours in Heaven*
   " *Will all be spent at Home!*"

THEY WENT AND TOLD JESUS.

St. Matt., chap. xiv., v. 12.

———————◆———————

Go and tell Jesus, when thine eye hath seen
  Dear hopes beheaded by the Tyrant, Death,
When reeds thou lovest pierce the hands that
    lean—
  Hear what He saith.

Go and tell Jesus. In the Gulf of Thought
  Alone, oh dive not! lest such root of
    bale
For pearls thou gather, as the Fisher brought
  In Eastern tale.

Go and tell Jesus. Turn each thought to
    prayer—
Nor smite frail crystal, where thy rebel
    Will
Cast by His word of power in ocean lair
    Lies wan and still.

Go and tell Jesus. Should'st thou yield it
    way,
Soon would the daring Essence upward loom,
And o'er thy cringing heart hold ruthless
    sway
From tower of gloom.

Go and tell Jesus, if from word arisen,
    In some weak moment forth one murmur
        steal,
He can the Giant-slave anew imprison
    With kingly seal.

Go and tell Jesus.   In His Wisdom lie
   All stores of solace.   When rude gales in-
      crease,
Ask, and His Love shall pour on passions high
   The oil of peace.

AWAKE, THOU THAT SLEEPEST.

"We are less dazzled by the light on awaking, if we have been dreaming of visible objects."—NOVALIS.

————————◆————————

SUNLIGHT unbroken is flooding the room,
Love's blesséd token, it banishes gloom;
Sleep is enchaining thee late in the day,
Friends are arraigning thee. Rise, nor delay !

Hast thou been dreaming of night scenes dark,
With no starlight gleaming on the wave-sprung
  bark ?
Then the splendors prevailing will dazzle thy
  sight
Through their fullness entailing a reflex of
  night.

10

Were thy dreams of the lustre that dwells at
    noon
Where vine leaves cluster o'er calm lagoon ?
Then, though landscape aerial must vanish
    away,
Will its colors ethereal blend well with full
    . day.

And refreshed through thy slumber, now may'st
    . thou rise
With no film to cumber unblenching eyes.
Let the sloth in his dullness grope dimly along—
In the strength of thy usefulness thou wilt be
    strong !

Thus, when thou art musing on heavenly
    things,
And thy heart's accusing a tremor brings,

Or a prescient self-pity, at thought of that
  hour
When the Jasper-walled City, with pearl-gate
  and tower,

Bears earthward the saintly in holiness white,
Lest thy blurred vision faintly shrink far from
  that Light
Lest taint of long sinning hang darkly on
  thee,
And hold thee from winning the glories to be.

Then lift, like an eagle, thy gaze on high ;
Can low dreams inveigle the heaven-drawn
  eye ?
Nay ! rise and determine on earth to seek
For the stainless ermine of spirits meek.

On that robe, Christ-woven, no fret or soil

Will, by Heaven's light cloven, work heart-
    recoil—

Fold thee now in its whiteness ! so Death shall
    bring

But familiar brightness of Home and King !

THE APOSTLES' CREED.

In a cavern of Judea, so the old traditions
run,
Were the twelve apostles gathered.   Stars
shine forth when day is done.
And that glorious constellation rose when vanished Christ, the sun.

Pleiad twin-group, soon to scatter where a
darkened world had need,
Bid a host of Helot nations in the Light of
Truth be freed,
And the hearts of millions mingle in their own
immortal Creed.

10*

"I believe in God the Father," first from mouth
    of Peter fell—
Mouth whose tremulous denial one Almighty
    look could quell,
And all fear of priest or Pilate from once-quail-
    ing heart expel.

Now his faith for aye emboldened through re-
    membrance of that look,
"Heaven and Earth, and Him their Maker,"
    in its far embracing took—
Nor Sanhedrim-scourge fast-falling for an hour
    its firmness shook.

Well might meek St. Andrew answer, "I be-
    lieve in Christ our Lord"—
He who left the great Fore-runner, and Mes-
    siah first adored—
Who, when cross-bound, spake of Jesus till
    his soul to glory soared.

"Through the Holy Ghost conceived, and of
    Mary, Virgin-born ;"
Witnessed one who saw dim vesture by the
    Man of Sorrows worn,
With a clear snow-brightness glisten, like fair
    Lebanon at morn.

Since that vision, pain and sorrow, and all pass-
    ing trials seem
With unearthly joy transfigured, through its
    ever-lucent beam—
Round King Herod's steel of vengeance soon in
    halo-light to gleam.

"Under Pontius Pilate suffered, and at length
    was crucified,"
Saith disciple loved of Jesus, who, long watch-
    ing near His side,
Saw from spear-thrust blood and water issue
    forth in blending tide.

'From that school of fearful anguish came the
  lesson, "God is love !"
Still on chaos-deep of sorrow broods for ever
  that bright dove !
"God is Love !" glad song-burst, chorused still
  through hierarchs above !

Philip then, for God's sight longing, "He de-
  scended into hell,"
Among spirits of the faithful till "the third
  day," gone to dwell ;
Then a Paschal Moon beheld Him "rise again"
  from rocky cell.

"He ascended into Heaven."—As the brother
  of our Lord
Said, "At God's right hand He sitteth," thro'
  his heart what memories poured
Of the Holy Child's meek wisdom while at
  Galilean board !

"And from thence again He cometh as the
    Judge of quick and dead"—
Faintest speck of doubt now sullies not the
    glow on Thomas shed
From bright scar of spear-and-nail wounds in
    his faithless view outspread.

Then Bartholomew, the guileless—"I believe
    in the Holy Ghost:"
He had seen the blue skies open, the ascending
    angel-host,
And the cloven flames that bickered through
    high noon of Pentecost.

Next the whilom son of traffic, chosen now for
    Gospel-scribe,—
"In One Holy Church," enfolding hearts re-
    deemed from every tribe,
"In communion of the saintly"—while they
    pray or praise ascribe.

Then St. Simon—"In forgiveness of all sins"
    through Jesus' name.
Soon by force of that fond message, he forgave
    both scorn and blame,
Praying long for cruel Persians, who to crucify
    him came.

"In the body's resurrection," spake Matthias,.
    "I believe,
Though sharp stones crush out my spirit, and
    but maiméd relics leave,
Thence the might of my Redeemer shall a form
    of power retrieve."

"And in Life—Life-everlasting," was the say-
    ing of St. Jude,
Vainly arrows of destruction, in his heart's
    blood soon embruéd,
Would arrest one hidden pulsing of that life
    through Christ renewed.

Then the holy Twelve, departing, wandered
    forth in search of men,
As true shepherds seek the straying, over
    mount and miry fen,
And glad voices of the rescued, through all
    ages, shout "Amen."

OLD AUTHORS.

WHEN youthful squire of yore
Paced up the moon-lit floor
Of dim cathedral, and in silence prayed
For grace to hold unstained
Leal faith and vow, till waned
The life ennobled by near accolade—

Dreamed he of camp-fire's jest—
Gay revel—lengthened quest
Of wild adventure for his knightly brand ?
Could thought of self defile
That watch in holy aisle,
With trophies bannered, won in Holier Land ?

Nay—from crusading tomb,
Low voices pierced the gloom,
Nerving the novice unto deeds like theirs;
And dint of Paynim stroke
On ancient visor woke
Dormant soul-valor, that all peril dares.

God's vassals we, who bow
In armor-vigil now,
Called from the camp of life in early prime
To hear, through long, lone hours,
Death knells from ivied towers,
And ghostly footfalls move in crypts of Time.

For us, it may be, wait
Bright embassies of state,
In realms of glory to our dreams unknown,
When touch of Kingly Hand
At dawn, shall bid us stand
Where stainless heroes ring our Monarch's throne.

11

But now, the night is drear,

How best may heart find cheer ?

With gladsome echoings from the world with-
     out ?

Not so—for tumult dies

Down, where a sufferer sighs,

As chapel-doors subdue the people's shout.

With words of men who braved

Long toil—long fears, and laved

Their wounded souls beside deep wells of
     life—

Who, Faith's ancestral lords,

Fought on through demon-hordes,

And for the Cross above it, hailed the knife ?

These shall our sponsors be—

The Truth they lived makes free,

Soul-sparks yet kindle from that deathless
     flint—

Nor heart in fear can melt,
Nor loneliness be felt,　.
While viewing on their mail Hope's moonlight
　　glint.

From thoughts in anguish penn'd
Long-buried saints yet send
A warmth magnetic, welding life with life—
　　And still, in dreariest hour,
　　Each clarion-phrase hath power
To brace the languid soul anew for strife.

I COUNT ONLY THE HOURS THAT SHINE.

INSCRIPTION ON A FLORENTINE SUN-DIAL.

WHEN first the morning light is seen
To glimmer on the dewy green,
And make the spider's filmy net
Like a bride's veil with diamonds set ;
And when the sun, in royal state,
Comes where cloud-courtiers grouping wait,
His beaming smile and look of grace
Given back from each attendant's face ;
All rosy morning hues are mine—
" I only count the hours that shine."

When the same sun hath mounted high
His palace stair-way in the sky ;

When, by his torrid force dismayed,
Tired cattle seek for leafiest shade,
And halls of marble fend the glare
From cheek and brow of ladye fair ;—
O ! then to me how dear his rays—
No cloud-roof intercepts my gaze
Upward in one uncheckered line :
" I only count the hours that shine."

At evening, upon Arno's stream,
When sun-glows shed their parting gleam,
And peasants meet for dance and glee
Beneath the branchful ilex-tree,
A maiden by her love forsaken—
A harp the minstrel will not waken—
A gathered rose flung idly by,
Are far less desolate than I ;
In vain the starry lamps combine—
" I only count the hours that shine."

If storms are gathering, and the change
Drift darkly down from mountain range,
While in thick forests, fertile vales,
All my beloved sunshine fails :
Then through long hours of gloom I wait
Till furious flood and gale abate,
Till the sun breaks o'er Vallombrose—
Warms the fair plains " where citron grows,"
And gilds the far-off Apennine—
" I only count the hours that shine."

Complainer ! when the page of life
Looks with black lettering mainly rife ;
When in some darling vision crost,
Every delight of Earth seems lost,
Review thy ranks of peaceful years,
Unscarred by pain, undimmed by tears ;
Number the mercies that are left,
Even though thou feel of all bereft,

And let the dial be thy sign—
"I only count the hours that shine."

And if thy soul, with anguish fraught,
Sink sadly, cheer thee with the thought
How soon each dusky sail will clear
In Heaven's unshadowed atmosphere !
Thou wilt remember all the love
Which led thee to thy home above ;
Thou wilt forget the trials here
That overcast thy short career ;
And sing, safe-moored in Port Divine—
"I only count the hours that shine !"

WEEPING MAY ENDURE FOR A NIGHT, BUT JOY COMETH IN THE MORNING.

WE lavish thought and prayer on those
Bowed low by grief, like guelder-rose
When hailstones through her garden-home are
    sweeping ;
Mute from our very awe, behold
The lightning's work on dewy fold
Of hearts ere while in warmth of summer
    sleeping.

Longs soul of friend, that shallow urn,
Thus to yield solace ?   How must yearn
Our Lord's deep Heart of Love when saints
    are weeping !
He whose Creative Breath first gave
Flowers unto Earth, each tear will save,
And smile it to a pearl in Heaven's sure keeping.

TO THE SUBTERRANEAN RIVER IN THE MAMMOTH CAVE OF KENTUCKY.

River, sad River! why dost thou stay
In a home unenlivened by glimmer of day?
Hast thou not learnt how thy sister streams
Move in the Sun's light and mirror his
    beams?
The caverns thou threadest are chilly and
    drear,
River, sad River! what dost thou here?

Over their waters gay vessels glide,
Banners gleam white as the gleaming tide,
Willows, like Naiads by clear, cool wave,
Bow, and luxuriant tresses lave—
But no royal pinnace, no graceful tree,
River, sad River! is glassed in thee.

Lightly the plashing of boatman's oar
Sounds on their banks when he rows from shore,
Seen in the moonlight their silvery spray
Glanceth like plumes beneath the south-wind's
    sway—
Thine oars waken murmurs of sorrow and fear,
River, sad River! what dost thou here?

Birds in their meadows blithe chorus sing,
And May-buds welcome the smile of spring,
There the young lambs with unweary play
Revel through Nature's holiday—
But thou hast no pastures nor fleecy flocks—
Tenant of lair in the heart of rocks!

Love's last token, so faintly blue,
Never hath drawn thy reviving dew—
And the spotless lily, that maiden queen—
Spreads on thy surface no tent of green,

Where are thy rushes and waving reeds,
Linked with renown of heroic deeds ?

No stately swan o'er thy bosom goes
With arched neck white as are wintry snows—
No fawn with lustrous yet timid eyes
Away from thy margin startled flies,
And childhood's voice, in its morning glee
Ringeth no musical notes for thee.

River, sad River, why wilt thou stay
Banished forever from vision of day ?
Break the strong arches, and let thy path
Rise like the Sea in its billowy wrath—
Soon woulds't thou shiver these bonds severe—
River, sad River ! oh, linger not here !

THE RIVER'S RESPONSE.

Tell me, if my caverns drear
Fill thee with this wondering fear,
Murmurer, why art *thou* here?

Why my lonely walls thou seekest
When through fields of verdure meekest
Flow the waves whereof thou speakest?

If the music thou hast heard
Of infant voice or singing bird
Hath thy heart's light surface stirred,

Wherefore list my sullen moan,
In a low funereal tone
From the caves beneath me thrown ?

Ah ! the sounds that o'er me roll,
Answer, with far-vibrant toll,
To the deeps within *thy* soul.   .

And no foam of torrent flashing
Through grim notch—nor angry lashing
Of the Sea on sand-hills dashing—

Nor the Lake in quiet vale
Shimmering under moonbeams pale,
Linked with legendary tale,

Round thy soul, with tendrils fine
Though their marvels loop and twine—
None shall clasp thee firm as mine.

12

Ere youth's joys are overcast,
Rarely will the impression last,
Caught from bright hues hurried past.

But meek life beneath a rod,
Understood of none save God,
Mirrors mine, in halls untrod.

Here because my Maker wills;
And this rough home under hills,
His wise planning best fulfills.

Never will I quit my cell;
Nor my soul-bewildering spell
To each careless zephyr tell.

'Tis enough that all, who ever
Sail a-down the Lonely River,
Shrine me in their souls forever.

THE BOTTOMLESS PIT

IN THE MAMMOTH CAVE OF KENTUCKY.

WILD way ! and wilder chasm !
 Our torch, with flickering ray,
Paints many a wierd phantasm
 On massy bowlders gray ; .
And, save our voices, all is still
As in a charnel-cavern chill.

A tiny cresset, hung
 Across the unfathomed deeps,
And slowly downward swung,
 With glow-worm lustre creeps ;
While rocks, that lie in giant rest,
Frown on their unfamiliar guest.

Faith's lamp, with quiet glow,
  (When all beside is gloom),
  Too faint the Past to show,
  The Future to illume,
Can thus all needful brightness shed
On souls through vault of shadows led.

Though scarce one gleam may fall
  On griefs of vanished days,
Though gloom envelope all
  Life's yet untravelled maze—
Move calmly on—thine hourly store
Of light sufficeth—ask no more!

CRADLE SINGING.

" So war es mir in der Wiege gesungen," is a proverbial expression for destiny in the north of Germany.

———————•———————

MOON-RAYS and vine-leaves light and shade
 were sending
 Through a still chamber. There, at close of
 day
A mother saw two glorious angels bending
 Over the cradle where her darling lay.

From crimson mist one form looked forth, and
 gayly
 Swung o'er the infant-brow a rosy crown :
White clouds the other veiled, and mosses daily
 Plucked by the Cross, her thorn-leaf made
 like down.

12*

"Give me thy child," sang one, "oh gentle
      mother !
For homes I haunt no sickening fears flit by,
None with feigned mirth a silent anguish
      . smother—
  All things are glad and fair when I am nigh.

" She shall be glad and fair, her buoyance win-
      ning
  Smiles from the saddest, through her mirth-
      strewn way ;
While ills that others feel, like fleece-clouds
      thinning
  At sight of sunshine, bring her brief dismay.

"Yield her to me, and I, with pleasures paving
      Her future path, the trust will truly keep,
And sow thick germs of light, whose increase
      waving,
  Thou in glad harvest may'st hereafter reap."

Ceased the sweet singing—and another measure
  Flowed from the white-robed form. A sense
    of calm
Came with the sounds, as when for dearest
    treasure
  All sobs are silenced by the burial-psalm.

" Give *me* thy babe, and though my name be
    Sorrow,
  And far my dwelling from the haunts of
    mirth,
She from my sterner training strength shall
    borrow :
  'Tis from crushed blossoms richest balms
    have birth.

" Tears she must shed alone her eyes will
    meeten
  To look on others' pangs with grieving
    glance,

Herbs she in twilight culls their gall-draughts
   sweeten,
   Through their dull nights her smiles, like
      fire-flies, dance.

"She shall have friends on high, gone home
   before her,
   For holier hands than hers in mine have lain;
And friends on earth, in heart of hearts who
   store her,
   Helped by her love through weariness and
      pain.

"And these will weave her an unfading gar-
   land,
   With joys unclustered, as of old the bees
Rifled true flowers of Sheban queen from far
   land,
   And left the false untouched in scentless
      ease.

"Give *me* thy babe !"   But here that mother's
  weeping
    Hushed the grief-angel, while her gaze for-
      lorn,
Saw on the lovely face, like rose-bud sleeping,
    The fearful shadow of the crown of thorn.

When bloom-hung boughs of joy so swiftly
    wither,
    How build her babe with these a shielding-
      booth ?
Since paths of grief with briars are strewn,
    how thither
    Doom the bright eyes and bounding feet of
      youth ?

Then, with bent knee, she cried : "Oh Lord, I
    rather
    Yield her to Thee. Thy will be done, not
      mine!

Be Joy or Grief her Guide, O wisest Fa-
    ther !
  Choose Thou her portion—only make her
    Thine !"

DIVINE SERVICE.

If once again to Thy fair Court
Of service, Lord, I might resort;
If mingling with the faithful there,
My voice went up in song and prayer,
And I could kneel at chancel-rail—
It may be heart and hope would fail
Less often, and Thy peace, like dew,
Lie on my way the whole week through.

O for a faith too firm to peer
For cloud-born joy or treasure here,
To grieve o'er earth-reeds broken now,
O'er dream of youth and film-spun vow—

Though, far as eye of sense may see,
Not one green hope is left for me,
'Tis Summer-land for loving heart
In every sojourn where Thou art !

Then make my soul Thy Temple, Lord !
Come and drive hence the chaffering horde,
Of eager thoughts whose murmurs fill
Porches and aisles against my will.
Thus, if no more within Thy Gate,
My feet on Thy dear service wait,
The long privation will be slight
With Thee for Altar, Priest, and Light !

DISSONANCE.

THE earth is full of discords, for men deem
    Each his own symbol sweetest. Selfish clang,
    Whelms holy sounds that first from Beth-
        lehem rang.
Firebells break harshly on melodious dream,
To sufferer's pillow brought by Christmas
    theme,
    Carolled in depth of midnight. Deafening
    bang
Of idol-service drowns the fakeer's pang
Crushed beneath car-wheels, while none heed
    his scream.
    Ah doleful Tuning-Time! our ears are
    stunned

13

With crossing clamors. Would our eyes might
        see
The Leader's rod uplifted, and his fund
  Of deep soul-music rise like snow rills sunned
'Neath Polar Summer.   So should Discord be
Flooded in harpings from the Crystal Sea !

HEART, WELL NIGH HOME.

Thy Life-cruise is ending,
  White crest of each wave
With swifter rush tending
  Home's ramparts to lave.
Then fear not the blending
  Of cloud, reef and foam—
Heart, well nigh home !

Not with soft moon-light
  Now glisten thy sails,
They are seen in full Noon-light,
  Soiled, threshed by storm-flails ;
But high as Love's Boon-light

Storm never clomb !
Heart, well nigh home.

Sea-wealth worth craving
　　Soothed not thy pride :
Dint of foes' graving
　　Paint will not hide.
But for Christ's saving
　　Help, ne'er hadst thou come
　　Heart, well nigh home.

.

Heart, therefore lay all
　　Low at his feet—
Years of betrayal,
　　Service how fleet !
Waiting there thine arrayal
　　Meet for Heaven's Dome,
　　Heart, well nigh home !

THE CHRISTIAN'S CHAIN.

WHAT is our Bible but a golden chain,
    With promises like pendant charms
For Faith to handle, strong to vanquish pain,
    Heal grief or soothe alarms?
Through a long ancestry, from saint to saint
    The noble heir-loom came,
Never by treason-forfeit or attaint,
    Allied with shame.

When gaze of thoughtful woman first is bent
    On antique jewels, will she say
Their worth lies wholly in the brightness lent
    To her own beauty?—Nay

Each sapphire splendor, amethystine gloom,
   Revives some olden tale
Of warrior's valor, or fond maiden's bloom,
   In death long pale.

Our jewels have their legends. Some have
      brought
   Mute odors from the Mount of Balm
To mourners faint with unavailing thought—
   From one beloved psalm
Come tones of hope, that trusting souls rehearse,
   Leaving their lodge of clay—
Prayer for renewal, through yon pleaded verse,
   Hath won its way,

The Word is precious. Well our own deep
      need
   Hath taught its value ; yet we love
To feel it link us with the Sacred Seed,
   Long housed in light above.

Fair memories lingering on from age to age,
   And names we never knew
Like vanished rose-leaves, haunt the Holy
     Page
   With fragrance true.

Whispers of blessing, wherewith martyrs stirred
   Dank air of catacomb and den !
Songs of meek praises, from apostles heard,
   With gyve-clank mingling then.
These hold we precious, and yet far more
     dear
   A Saviour's parting prayers—
No solemn utterance of bard or seer—
   Hath power like theirs.

One Family in Heaven and Earth. His hand
   Grasps our gem-laden treasure still,
And weakest touches from His own frail band
   Still rouse the immortal thrill.

Friends ! who that force electric once have felt,
  Round it more closely curl
Your clasp, nor let the scoff corrosive melt
  One priceless pearl.

"LIKE HIM, FOR WE SHALL SEE HIM AS HE IS."

1 John, chap. 3, v. 2.

Weary of self and sin,
　'Tis well to look away
From inward evil—outward sin—
　To Christ's Appearing-Day:

For when He shall appear,
　My cup of life will brim
With Love's pure wine, uncloyed by Fear,
　And I shall be *like Him*.

Like Him! My thoughts that swoop
　Afar with falcon's wing,

Then round His throne will meekly group,
   And there glad praises sing.

Like Him! My wayward lips,
   Touched by Death's cleansing coal,
Shall veil no more, in half eclipse,
   Deep workings of the soul.

Like Him! No wilful prayer
   Will soar on pinion strong,
But to enhance my heart's despair,
   And beat at Heaven's gate long.

Like Him! No faultful deeds,
   To fence of duty blind,
Rise in rank growth—unsightly weeds
   From soil of godless mind.

Like Him! My restless will—
   No longer prone to carp—

Shall at His bidding softly thrill,
  As thrills an air-moved harp.

While Joy's long dormant flower
  Blooms, with no stain to dim
Its broad unfolding, from the hour
  When I shall be LIKE HIM !

LEGEND OF ST. CHRISTOPHER.

LONE among rocks the Giant lay—
His might of soul inert as they—
Viewing broad billows ebb away.

Yet wave and rock, from boyhood's hour,
Thrilled him with sense of kindred power
Like wave to lash—like sea-cliff tower;

And if around Love's sun-lit isle
Thought-currents gleamed in joy awhile,
Soon fell the spring-flood—ceased the smile.

" The strong sea knows his path," he said,
  " Is ruled by yon calm moon;

But the surgings of my soul, unled,
  For channels importune ;
I tire of winter—snow bespread—
  As I tire of summer noon.
Glad sea ! with life-rule traced on high—
Glad moon ! whose light may wane, not die—
Ye have your task-work—none have I."

Lifting then his stalwart length,
In full majesty of strength,
  Forth Phoros fared,
Craving, for the arm and breast
That in work alone found rest—
Service of Earth's mightiest
  King, with power unshared.

Stately palace wins his eye,
  Stately chief his prowess viewing,
Notes how in the brave arms lie
  Strength and skill for foes' subduing,

14

While the child-heart longs to serve,
Nor from loyal faith will swerve ;
Well may the warrior-monarch hail
   His coming, dream of foes unhorsed,
And of souls threshed out from their fleshly
     mail,
   Like grain from its shell in autumn forced,
By that massive human flail.

And then heart of Phoros bounded
   With gleeful sense of gain ;
No more from dull inaction hounded
   To effort wild as vain—
Hope scaled the hill-peak viewed so long,
And toil and honor crowned the strong.

One morn there came a herald, sent
   With speed from a lonely village, where
Marauders in the midnight went
To rifle sleeping shepherd's tent ;

Nor might their vulture talons spare
One living child, one matron bent,
  One old man's meek white hair.

Listened the king, with a wrathful brow :
" Satan our world is walking now,"
  Spake one of his valiant men ;
And the royal hand at that word of bale
Signed the cross, and his cheek grew pale—
  But Phoros questioned then :

" Whence this Satan, noble sire ?
  I had deemed thee first of all
  Kings who this world keep in thrall—
Canst thou fear another's ire !"
    " Ask me not," his lord replied,
      " Learning will but grieve thee."
    " Nay," the stalwart vassal cried,
      " Tell me, or I leave thee."

And the unwilling Chieftain press'd
Fear of Satan's power confessed.

Faded then his vassal's dream,
Faded all his fond esteem,
Only to the Mightiest, he
Pledged his own might loyally.
Sadly grasping sword and shield
Moved he to the avenging field ;
There beneath his falchion fell
Mowed like grass, the Infidel—
But when the war-tide ceased to roll,
Forth from the camp Phoros stole.

Soon in a lonely mountain-glen
The Giant found the Foe of men ;
Willingly his guileless thought
Bowed before a strength long sought ;

Slender parley, brief soul siege
Needed ere he hailed his Liege.

And meekly he followed the Prince of Air
Through wild-wood pathways, by wild brute's
   lair,
Till a Cross upreared on a bleak hill-side
Imaged the love of the Crucified ;
  Aside the Demon flew,
Nor paused for tangle, brier or fosse,
Till far from Shadow of the Cross,
  His new-found thrall he drew.

"Wherefore this haste ?" Phoros spake ;
"Plainer yon hill-path than briarful brake."

"Little boots it, friend, to know—
  Ivy-crown, perchance, I'd weave thee"—
But Phoros cried—" Not so !
  Tell me, or I leave thee !"

"Once with the Being sculptured there
Long time I wrestled, unaware
What inborn strength enshrouded lay—
What dauntless soul, in sheath of clay !
At last he fell.   In triumph reigned
My star awhile.   That fall was feigned :
Soon from my grasp the Christ arose ;
And still we meet as lifelong foes—
Here let the hateful memory close."

"Greater then his might than thine,"
    Mused Phoros—"Master Mine !"

"Heed him not, my vassal true,
I have realms he never knew ;
There long years of bliss await thee,
There shall smiles of pleasure sate thee,
    Warm as sunshine, bright as dew."

But the soul he deemed enmeshed,
As with wine of Life refreshed,

Rose, and calmly turned away
From that losel in affray,
Toward the Prince who won the day.

———————•• ◆ ••———————

In the heart of silent forest
  Knelt an agéd man and prayed,
Pilgrims when their need was sorest,
  Sought for help that home-like glade.
Him Phoros told—" To none
But the strongest Monarch under Sun
  Are my vows of service paid.
I have learned through wanderings long,
Christ is strongest of the strong ;
But His Court is far away.
None I seek the road can say ;
All its waymarks are too dim ;
Lead me, Father, unto Him."

"Not with eye of sense, my Child,
　　Canst thou view the Undefiled :
　　Lordly growth and might of limb
　　Form not offerings meet for Him.
　　He no battle service needs ;
　　Dearer to His heart are sighs,
　　If from lowly thoughts they rise,
　　Than archangels' valiant deeds.
　　Turn from haunts of Earth aside,
　　Bow in prayer thy own vain pride ;
　　Through long fastings watch and kneel,
　　Till thy Lord Himself reveal."

　　" I will not fast to lose
　　　　Strength by my Maker given ;
　　I can not pray and muse
　　　　All day, on far-off Heaven.
Long lonely hours are too drear a ban ;
Bid me toil for this Saviour, thou saintly
　　man."

" Where in many a dangerous eddy
   Snake-like, yon deep river rolls,
Strength of thine, perchance, may steady
   Failing strength of feeble souls.
Thither hasten, hourly aiding
   All in want or fear who cry,
Shrink not then from midnight wading
   Lift thy heart to Christ on high."

Soon from river-bank uprooting
   For his staff tall trunk of palm,
Passed he his life in suiting
Cordial help to weakling's qualm—
Guarded by his fearless footing,
   Frailest pilgrim crossed in calm.
Christ the while, on earth who served,
Watched, well-pleased, the strength so
     nerved
Lowliest task-work to fulfill,
Faithful, though in darkness still.

Watched the love, that spring-like welled,
Nor from tiny cup once held,
Deemed the poor man's thirst all quelled.

One night the flood was foaming high,
And harsh winds told of tempest nigh ;
While Phoros mused with many a sigh
On his so long-deferred reward,
On craved-for vision of His Lord.
For heavy and dark was the load of sin ;
And wilder the warring his soul within,
Than moan and shriek of the swollen Linn.

Lo ! a faint, half-whispered cry
Fell on his ear as a babe were nigh,
And the Giant marvelled—Had he slept ?
When again it rose.—From their pallet leapt

The strong limbs swiftly ; his staff is ta'en
And forth he plunges through blinding rain.
Again that cry.—On the bank a child
Watches the torrent, seething wild,
" Wilt thou bear me over, Friend ?" it cried ;
" Mine errand lieth on yonder side."

Then Phoros raised the fair young form,
And turned his face unto flood and storm.
Scarce hath one firm foot felt the wave,
When tempest-voices loudlier rave,
And the child-burden presseth sore,
Strong though his arm, ere half-way o'er.

Higher yet the storm-wave surges,
Tireless yet the storm-wind scourges,
And the palm-staff, tried of old,
Finds in shifting sand no hold,
While the child's arm, round him curled,
Weighs, as though he bare a world.

Fails the prowess once so vaunted—
Fails the cheer till now undaunted—
In this struggling shall he sink ?
One more step, for need is urgent !
Yet another—and emergent
Falls he by the channel's brink ;
Borrowing for his fearful burthen
From the rough bank, cradle earthen.
Panting faintly, " Child thy name !
Fair thou art, and slight of frame ;
But wayfarer never came
Near this ford, whose clasp could twine
Round me with a force like thine !"

Parted then the dusk night-cloud ;
Hushed the winds their quarrel loud ;
But on turf the moon-beams lay
Not with half so pure a ray,
As, in mingled power and grace,
Shines around that Infant-Face,

Made the rough bank holy ground—
Holy, with a Saviour found.

Soon to Love's most loving tone
Changed the child's appealing moan.
Planting, at its word, his palm
In the damp earth, buds of balm
From the well-worn staff arose ;
And sweeter dates than Hermon grows.
Formed the feathery palm-leaves fair
Coronal for trunk so bare ?
Feebly could their flush compare
With the glad thoughts that enring
Heart unhoping, whilst full Spring
Comes with coming of its King !

Touched, transfigured through the sight,
Life and death alike grow bright.
Though Heaven's glory lure away—
He for pilgrim's help can stay ;

15

Earth's mad storms may round him fly—
Henceforth he can dare and die.

Ere long he learned how Lycian hordes
Drenched in the blood of saints their swords,
And thither led by mystic cords,
Phoros sought the idol-lanes
Of Samos, red with martyr-stains.
Thrice happy if his tones of cheer,
Gladdening erewhile wayfarer's ear,
Might now with hopes enheartening guide
Those before whom, in heavier tide,
Flowed the Death-Torrent, dark and wide.

Rained heathen smitings on his face?
He smiled back: "But for Jesus' grace
Well would mine arm avenge each blow;
But Christian hearts no malice know!"

Then to a throne of judgment near,
  The martyr's stalwart friend they led;

Their puny kingling swooned in fear,
  And cried, " Thy name, O man of dread!"
Answered his captive, low and clear :

"Phoros, Bearer—called of yore
From burthens that with ease I bore ;
Till carrying One than all Earth fairer,
I learned of Him a nobler aim,
And won from Him my nobler name :
Now in His martyrs' love a sharer—
Christopher—Of Christ the Bearer."

Storm of menace, jeer and blows
Round him with that word arose :
But his robe of faith he held
Closer while the heathen yelled.
Then temptation's summer-call
Would with song and bloom enthrall,
Till, subdued, strong heart should fall :—
Thong or threat, or floral chain

Might not win for altars vain
From his palm one incense-grain.

Kneeling ere the headsman's stroke
Loosed his soul from fleshly yoke,
Christopher the silence broke :
" Saviour, if weak pilgrims tire
Through the force of flood and fire,
Earth-quake, storm, or thunder-peal,
Hear Thou ! when the tremblers kneel,
Thinking on my dreary case—
Dreary, till Thy Glorious Face,
Beamed on more than midnight gloom.
And while, trusting in Thy grace,
They the help I found retrace,
May Thy love their faith illume,
And all shadows, dark to see,
From Thy radiant Presence flee !"

NOTE.—This legend, evidently allegorical, has been called
the Pilgrim's Progress of mediæval times, and was very pop-
ular among citizens and peasantry.

THE RAINBOW ON THE RAILWAY.

On, on, through swamp and tangle,
With brain-bewildering jangle,
Fierce cry and fiercer wrangle,
   The Fire-Steed flew :
Past Cypress veiled in mosses
(Long worn for greenwood losses)
That over shiny fosses
   Dull shadows threw :
O'er rice-marsh dankly seething
Past poison vines up-wreathing,
From loveliest blossoms breathing
   Most fatal dew—

15*

Where sparkle-boughs shone varnished
O'er pools with lilies garnished,
And tiny runnels, tarnished
Through heaps of pine,
High boles once gaily fringing,
Then bronzed by camp-fire's singeing
And now the clear waves tinging
  With tawny wine.
Past wood-scenes borne thus lightly
Through din and smoke unsightly
To me a sense came brightly
  Of Care Divine.

For, spite of haste and whirling,
Like sound of maelstrom swirling,
Where the white steam rose curling
  A Sun-Bow lay,
Rich-hued as some that tarry,
Where beams and dew-drops marry,
And heaven's bright flashes carry

Through cataract spray :
Full-arched as others, glowing
  On men for dear life rowing,
When summer storms are going
    From ocean-bay.

Sign of God's sure befriending,
Frail heart from ill defending,
Thy silent lesson blending
    With that fierce din,
Said " Thus, in scenes of squalor,
Can Faith, with cheery valor,
Turn its bright prism on pallor
    Of toil and sin ;
Thus too, our God,—if duly,
Through all Earth's noise unruly,
We seek and serve Him truly,—
    Gives peace within."

SUSPENSE.

WORSE ordeal far than gloomiest fate,
That life, wherein the sentence "Wait!"
Seems from each hour inalienate.

When vulture-fancies scent from far
A coming fight; and sound of war
Thrills with new pangs the long-healed scar;

To stand in day-dawn's blissful hush,
Fearing, ere night, the winnowing rush
Of tempest wings all joy may crush.

To feel the heart a prisoner, pent
As in old tower where sunlight sent,
Through seven high lattices, content.

Content soon lost in doubt and fear;
When, one by one, each lattice clear
Did dim and all opaque appear.

So fade youth's hopes and visions—fade
The gentle forms by love arrayed
In light which noon of twilight made.

The joys that sprang when life began
Evanish, till we faintly scan
Day's glimmer through one narrow span;

And waiting, watch the dark Death-Wall
Come nearer, nearer; while a pall
Of terror holds the heart in thrall.

Nay, captive, nay! Unviewed of thee
Beyond that Wall, with golden key,
One at whose smile all shadows flee,

Waits till thy vision, purged from sin,
May strength, through grief's anointing, win
To bear the light His love lets in.

When from Life's often-clouded day
The last dear splendor dies away,
Closing thine eyelids, meekly pray

That He would pierce the fold of sense
With warmth from Heaven, whose glow intense
Can still the shiver of suspense.

Thus when His voice at length is heard
Calling to freedom long deferr'd ;
Heart, hope, and love unsepulchred,

Shall sigh no more in chains of care—
Shall breathe no more a prisoner's prayer,
Sure of all bliss—with Jesus there.

THE LESSON OF GIDEON.

JUDGES, chap. viii., v. 1-7.

A PLEA FOR MISSIONS.

To our homes, lo ! the Champion of Israel
   draws nigh,
While his valiant three hundred move wearily
   by ;
And rich though their trophies, their number
   no more,
Than a gleaning of grapes when the vintage is
   o'er.

And slender the service He claims at our
   hands,
For the few who thus foray in far border-
   lands :

Rich purple-hued raiment, soft cushions and
    pelf,
Were unmeet for His chosen—unsought by
    Himself.

We dwell with our people:—through alien
    morass,
Lone defile, or jungle, in silence they pass ;
Bright soil of the desert their sandals may burn,
But the heart-glow is brighter—they will not
    return.

From the "faint yet pursuing," withhold we
    the bread,
Which lacking, they fall in their armor, unfed :
While our prayers and our love should be with
    them, as wine,
When all that is cheering, for Christ, they
    resign.

Oh shame on our self-love ! Through inner-
    most room

Of each silken pavilion floats whisper of doom,

Like the rustling of wings ere all happiness
    flee,

"Gifts held from my servants are held back
    from Me."

Up, friends ! at the warning, from pillow of
    rest !

To pile for your Chief and His chosen our
    best ;

Lest leaving those brave hearts to press on for-
    lorn,

With briars, when He cometh, our own hearts
    be torn.

16

RACHEL, LADY RUSSELL.

I.

"Whatever below God is the object of our love, will at some time or other be the matter of our sorrows."—LETTERS OF LADY RUSSELL.

HER rose of love unfolded, bud and bloom
   Perfect in beauty, while the Master's look
   Watched with approval. Then from garden-
      nook
Of home His hand removed it. Was there
      room
In the close leaves for canker? Would per-
      fume
   Be lost in world-born vapors, that He took
   The rose so roughly, and with wild winds
      shook
Buds left yet lingering, hedged in ivy gloom?

Ah ! bliss of Earth is but a plant whose seed,

Perennial in Heaven's tropic soil, doth need*

Yearly renewal in our chillier clime.

We weep o'er flowers removed ere winter's
rime ;

And by our weeping blinded, fail to heed

How safe their crystal shield from blasts of
Time !

II.

"Has the prisoner any one to aid him in taking notes ?" asked the judge. "My wife is here, my lord, to do it," said the accused.

HISTORY OF ENGLAND.

She can not stay to weep while voice or pen

Yields chance to aid him. Tears now fleck

Her bark's clear sunshine, but with him on
deck

They will seem luminous hereafter, when

Both voice and pen are failures, and fierce men

* Dr. Livingston discovered a species of cotton-plant in the interior of Africa, which was not an annual, as with us, but, once sown, continued to flourish for years.

Have hailed with ready zeal a tyrant's beck;
When she, the lone survivor of that wreck,
Peers o'er the waste for seas beyond her ken,
Where floats in peace her dear lord's caravel.
Heart of true woman ! faithful to the last,
All selfish pangs one smile of love can quell—
Not till that smile hath vanished, hurrying fast,
Can after-tides of woe her spirit cast
On shores where hoarse gales murmur "Is it
   well ?"

III.

"I was too rich in possessions while I possessed him: all relish now
is gone."—LETTERS OF LADY RUSSELL.

Her heart, resplendent once as royal hall   .
   Where Joy was reigning, views him now de-
      throned ;
   While the soiled blazonries and shields he
      owned
Bear, in debasement, witness to his fall.
Grief, the new monarch, sits for coronal

'Midst dark-robed peers, and scutcheons
     darker toned.
His sad-voiced champion hath a challenge
     droned
'Gainst all usurpers, and with gauntlet-call,
  Waits for defiance, where no thought defies.
In hours of agony alone we learn
  What solemn depth our being underlies,
Though every wish for that old sovereign yearn,
  Though loyal fancies would in rapture rise,
Joy's reign of sunlight never can return.

IV.

"My glass runs low. The world does not want me, nor I want
that."—Lady Russell.

" I should have been afraid of such a woman as Lady Rachel; it would
have been too awful. There are pieces of china very fine and beautiful,
but never intended for daily use."—Sydney Smith.

Yet years of life await her.   Sorrow kills
  In ballads only or antique romance,
  And the close-linkéd mail of circumstance

Arms her for living, with firm corslet stills
Each mad death-longing. Mirth of childhood fills
   The home made silent.   Youth's untroubled
     dance
May not be fettered by her tearful glance ;
Nor will she quail anew from death-bed ills,
   Braced for all anguish, having known the
     worst.
   And sad hearts love her, since their bitter
     thirst
Her hand from living well will meekly slake.
   Let mirthful natures deem her heart in-
     hearsed,
And shrink from one so chastened. God will take
Her closer 'neath His wing whom men forsake.

V.

"It is reasonable to believe our friends find that rest we yet but hope
for."—LADY RUSSELL.

Keen Death air rises in the ungenial East,
   And floats o'er graves where lie our holy dead

With feet turned eastward, waiting for the
Tread,
That startles worldlings from their wassail-
feast
To fears, like lightning, felt when looked for
least.
But dawn brings glory. Christ His guests
hath led
To the fair chamber, Peace, whose pleasant bed
Fronteth the sunrise. There, no rose leaf
creased,
They rest till morning. Shall an acorn
guess
What far capacities of height and shade,
Like growth unseen, its dull-hued sides com-
press ?
How from one hour of joy can heart o'er-
weighed
With care, the brancaful growth of blessedness
Foretell, on southward slope of Eden's glade ?

PARTING.

Now I have lost whom most fondly I love,
To-day's wind hath tost thee afar, my own
    dove !
And still to my vision repeats thy dear smile,
In gentlest derision—" 'Tis but for awhile ;
How foolish our weeping ! Like infants at
    play,
Recoiling and peeping, we part for one day."

Ah Love ! through each parting, too brief for
    a tear,
Wild May-Bes are darting, winged missiles of
    fear,

That hint, as they hurtle, how venom of
 asp
May be sheltered in myrtle, and sting ere I
 clasp ;
How often veiled dangers which Love would
 avert,
Unnoticed by strangers, work horror and hurt.

" I fear where I should not."   Thy voice, too
 hath said—
" Since true spirits could not by Death be
 unwed
On dew-drops if Light fall, and lift one on
 high,
While in flower-leaf till nightfall another may
 lie ;
Both upwards are fleeing—both worship one
 Sun,
And lapse in His Being when earth-life is
 done."

I doubt not the saying, yet daily my prayer
Seeks thy Sun-Life's delaying, till I too am
    there.
If angels accost thee, respond not, mine own !
From my Nile, had I lost thee, the lotos were
    gone ;
Whose deep root holds firmer when gales prove
    its power ;
'Tis therefore I murmur to miss thee an hour.

"EXCEPT THE LORD BUILD THE HOUSE THEY LABOR IN VAIN THAT BUILD IT."

My cottage lay in ruins—tempest-torn,
 I need not tell you how.
Fierce winds the fragile walls had earthward
  borne,
 And battered each green bough.
Enough. I must repair the tenement,
 Elsewhere I could not go ;
And pitying friends came round me, with intent
 Their counsel to bestow.

First Fancy o'er my garden-plot would pore,
 With·promises and plan
To make my dwelling firmer than before :
 But when the work began,

Her levers failed one beam or plank to move,
    Fashioned from baseless air;
And her most choice materials did but prove
    Kaleidoscopic ware.

Then Skill showed plainly how, with hail o'er-
        borne,
    The slender sides and roof
Yielded to pressure, yet, less roughly worn,
    Had been tornado-proof.
Opined, with stancheons new—with careful
        latch,
    And ivy-bands to climb
From porch to gable, linking sill with thatch,
    The House might last my time.

Next, Love and Patience came with tender smile,
    And yet more tender care;—
Sought in safe order stones afresh to pile,
    Cementing all with prayer.

Storms of an hour some finished portions felled,
    Oft, when the work looked best—
Still toiled they on, by failures unrepelled,
    With beaver's dauntless breast.

Faith from our council long had held aloof—
    Then, while we paused in fear,
Unfolding drawings with far loftier roof
    Than our poor means could rear,
She cried, "Oh waste not wealth of hand or
        brain,
    This ruined home to gild,
All work of man's devising will be vain,
    Unless Jehovah build.

"'Tis now when strongest, but a captive'
        cell;
    Soon must thy soul depart,
In brighter mansion for awhile to dwell,
    Not built through mortal art.

Yet in thine absence, from the mould and dust,
    Another home shall spring :
There will thy Guardian, faithful to His trust,
    The ancient tenant bring.

"Then find thy solace in yon hastening hour,
    Let Love and Patience think
That Hill-born breezes come with holier power
    Through each unlovely chink.
And though thy neighbor's barns with brim-
    ming sheaves
Of health and hope be filled,
Dwell thou unmurmuring beneath broken eaves,
    Till thy Redeemer build !"

THOMAS FULLER ON PINS.

Once, after lengthened musing,
    Thus wrote a quaint divine:
How marvellous the using
    Of pins on raiment-fine !

In size and worth how trifling !
    A moment's careless boon—
Yet rough winds would be rifling
    Our robes without them soon.

How vast their glittering levies !
    Replenished year by year ;
Each day, through seam and crevice ;
    What thousands disappear !

And swiftly we replace them,
  Unheeding earlier store,
Gone where no eye can trace them—
  Alas ! I marvel more

At men, so brave and sightly,
  Yet in their Maker's Hand
Held but as pins that slightly
  Secure some household band.

Brightly their busy millions,
  Gleam forth, then through the floor
Of this world's gay pavilions
  Sink, and are seen no more.

Missed for how brief a season !
  Mourned by a sorrowing few ;
Forgotten soon by reason
  Of mourners buried too.

No vision may behold them
   On dark path while they go ;
No human grief enfold them
   Save with a passing show.

Glad thought ! Though friends have van-
      ished
   Like pins from earthly view,
God will recall His banished,
   And bid them shine anew !

      17*

SECOND CAUSES.

When some great grief descends
   On the prone heart, nor lends
A loop-hole through which light may peer,
   While tiniest stone, once kept
   Secure, by wise adept,
Had all reversed and ruin were now near—
We feel what weights of woe depend
On frailest hair-line that a breath might
      rend.

   Might rend, but may not, since
   A Hand too firm to wince
For man's wild menace, clasps the knot

Where myriad films entwine,
And myriad wills combine
To body forth His will who shapes our lot :
How then should skill or tortuous plans
Elude the Look, that all wierd influence scans?

And could our mole-eyes trace
Those issues to their place
In God's true foresight, hushed were then
All murmurs. Hearts would lie
Low at His feet, and cry,
" In love Thou didst it, Loving Lord of Men !
Our quivering lips yet kiss Thy rod—
Our worn feet press no paths, by Thee un-
      trod."

It was a heathen chief,
Who heard thy tale of grief,
And dashed to earth in ire his battle-blade,

With vow : " Had I been there—

I, with my own Franks—ne'er

Should the meek Victim on that cross have
  staid !"

Clovis would Roman spears have braved,

To leave the broad world and himself unsaved!

THE BUTTERFLY.

In the neighborhood of Lake Champlain, a beautiful insect was so attracted by a lady's singing, as to follow her for some distance, suffer itself to be caught, and finally die in her hands.

———————

BUTTERFLY ! thy wings are bright
As they flutter in the calm sunlight,
And through this fair Sylvan scene,
Waft thee, like an insect-queen,
Born her royal home to make
Close beside the lilied lake,
With its murmuring waves to play,
And merrily pass her life's short day.

What though the summer time be brief,
Thy plumes will fade before the leaf;

What though in regions far from here
Thou mightest sport 'neath skies more clear,
Breathe the perfume of countless roses,
And sip the dew each bud uncloses—
Would it be a more joyous lot
Than to dwell in this sequestered spot,
Watching the wavelets kiss the shore—
Flitting in sunshine till life be o'er.

Sweet are the songs our dear one sings—
Thou hast folded thy gorgeous wings,
And sunk in delight, on her arm art thou
    found,
Fearing to lose one magic sound.
Where didst thou learn to love the song,
And follow the minstrel's steps so long ?
Hast thou listened to elfin lays
Sung at eve in the moon's pale rays ?
Shaken off morning sleep to mark
Voice of linnet or carol of lark ?

Or hath the swell of this tiny sea
Wakened thy sense of melody ?

Ah ! the burst of that noble air
Is more than thy fragile frame can bear :
It has trembled awhile with responsive thrill
To each plaintive cadence, each lingering trill,
Till in mournful pleasure, delicious pain,
Thou hast sighed out thy life with the last
    refrain.

Often some gay saloon has rung
With glad applause as the lady sung,
While a flush of pleasure, a gathering tear,
Proved the accents of praise sincere ;
But never till now hath her charméd lay
Stolen the listener's life away !

Well would it be if the wayward heart
In thy wild devotion had no part !

Well, fair insect, if none save thee
Fronted the perils of ecstacy !
Vain idol-lovers ! we weave our bliss
From the shining films of a world like this,
Where the sweetest voice and the dearest
    smile
Only are ours for a little while.
Soon our golden image shows feet of clay,
Our gossamer treasure floats far away,
And then we long to lie down and die—
Sharing thy fate, poor butterfly !

SANS PEUR ET SANS REPROCHE.

"BLAMELESS and fearless." With banner all
    bright,
Forth to far battle once hurried brave knight,
Held it unspotted through War's gory rush,
As a white peak whence paleth the long vesper
    flush.

"Blameless and fearless" our ensign shall be,
For liegemen of Jesus the Sinless are we ;
No guilt on the conscience, no fear in the soul
May palsy their might whom His Love hath
    made whole.

18

"Blameless and fearless" that legend's brave
  tone
Need not ring among ranks of the stalwart
  alone ;
A child's arm through hole of the sea-dyke
  thrust down
Once saved from their death-doom the hosts of
  a town.

"Blameless and fearless." If legion of foes
Round the eremite soul in Earth's wilderness
  close,
While leaning on Jesus, it watcheth all fears,
With the smile of an infant at glancing of
  spears.

For the Blameless hath lifted the load of our
  blame—
The Fearless through Valley of Horrors once
  came,

And scattered bright germs in each furrow of
    night,
For those who have loved Him, to harvest in
    Light.

HOMELESSNESS.

FORTH among strangers. Ah! unwelcome word!
    Drear penalty incurred
By many a mourner, since the first frail pair
Saw that dear Eden Love had made so fair,
    Flame-barred against their prayer ;
While the vast expanse they were free to range
    Looked desolate and strange.

Forth among strangers. To the young in heart
    Tired of inactive part,
Change seems but gladness—alien scenes arise,
Clad in the rosy mist of morning skies ;
    When inexperienced eyes
Turn gaily to the Future's brightening shore,
    And grieve for home no more.

But when Life's glow hath faded, and the soul
    Cares less for shining goal,
Than for some bosky shelter by the way,
To shield for dust-worn eyes the glare of day,
    And cheat Care of his prey ;
Change *will* look dark, though in its ebon chest
    Grim-carven, jewels rest.

Pleasant the parlor-brightness, when at eve,
    Unwearying fire-gnomes weave
Their radiant pictures, ready for a gaze
Skilled in red hieroglyphs. More bright the
    rays,
    Which 'neath fond eye-lids blaze
A beacon-welcome, unto look that knows
    What spell that kind glance throws.

But sad and heartless to go forth alone,
    Silent as Theban stone

Dragged by rude Fellah over desert-sand,
Left undeciphered, till some gentler hand
　　Half trace its mystic brand :
Then from brief contact, pass with uncon-
　　　cern—
　　This task is hard to learn !

Peace, murmuring spirit ! Did thy Lord com-
　　　plain
　　Of far more bitter pain
Borne in thy service ? Changes though thou
　　　see,
What home so full of joy can ever be,
　　As that He left for thee ?
While thy dull nature, unto earth akin,
　　Shrinks not as His from sin.

He chose a manger for His infant head—
　　He borrowed his last bed.

Yet hath He power and wisdom—Were it best,
Proud palace at His beck would claim thee guest,
   And give thee longed-for rest.
Go! with His promise cheer each painful mile—
   And wait thy Home, awhile.

"WE KNOW NOT WHAT WE SHALL BE."

"My knowledge of that life is small,
The eye of faith is dim—
But 'tis enough that Christ knows all,
And I shall be with Him."   BAXTER.

————————◆————————

My day of dreariness and mist
    At length, they tell me, nears the close—
No cloud of flame and amethyst
    A radiance o'er its ending throws:
I shall not leave the plain of fight
With shield undarkened, sword of might,
And stainless plume of conquest dight.

Slow-moving, as a pilgrim may,
    Too faint with travel, blind with tears,
To sorrow o'er his disarray,
    Or note how fast the home-light wears,

Through weary brain, this thought alone
Rings with a restful curfew-tone—
Love leads me, though in paths unknown.

Yet long unused, from lowland roads
    To gaze on Heaven, I can not scan
Through glass of power, the calm abodes
    Whose sapphires blaze, unseen of man ;
Counting their bulwarks, pure as gold,
Their gem foundations manifold,—
Enough for me what Christ hath told !

Nor, should I reach them, can I tell
    If all the pleasures longed for here,
And loved ones lost, with song's rich swell
    Shall give me welcome, guest and peer :
Or if my soul her lamp must trim,
The Bridegroom meet in night-paths dim,
And find her bliss, alone with Him.

Hearts, to whose love no toil seems hard,
   No grief o'erwhelming, need not grope,
As gropes my faith, so long debarred
   From aught save clutch of earthward slope ;
Unblenching while they front Heaven's glow.
Unto my Saviour's feet I go—
Me it sufficeth, if He know !

For He hath promised, man nor fiend
   Shall from His holding wrench apart
The feeblest who on Him hath leaned,
   And stilled heart-tremblings near His heart.
Soul, through long years Christ's willing thrall,
His liegemen throng yon Palace-wall—
Why shrink from Death, the Seneschal ?

SORROW AND CONSOLATION.

LONG the world a sunlit screen hath woven,
  Sorrow's realm to veil in twilight dun;
As a mine by midnight toilers cloven,
  All unnoticed shuns the beaming Sun.

From that world's gay homes her dwellings
      vary;
  They who lease them breathe an altered air :
Mirthful beings of these shades are wary,
  Deeming naught save wailing echoes there.

Thence if poet's hand the lichens gather,
  Singing of their soft grey hues the while,
Rarely finds he listeners.   All would rather
  Hear of blossoms whereon noonbeams smile.

Silent Realm of shadows uninviting !
  Freemen of thy Cities none would be,
Yet from cressets these dull pathways lighting,
  Solace falls on some who cannot flee.

Sorrow's world, like sister worlds, revolveth
  Calmly through far space on balanced poles :
And auroral light around them solveth
  Life's dark symbols to reliant souls.

From the North the brilliant message coming
  Calls to every mourner—" Time is short,
Care not for chill ice-breath, joy benumbing,
  While thy sails are set for golden Port."

And from Southern Pole a quiet whisper
  Saith more softly—" 'Tis thy Father's will,
Cannot loving heart of infant lisper
  Trust a Father's love to work no ill ?"

Sorrow's seal of consolation beareth
    Like devices, won from each far Pole ;
Sorrow's 'scutcheon for supporters weareth
    These, as pillars lifting high her scroll.

But a trainéd eye alone can read them :
    Who the heraldry of grief will scan,
Till his fond hopes fall, with none to heed them ;
    Till he moves, a lonely, sorrowing man ?

Then its legends bring, on breath of blessing,
    Thoughts to gayer spirits full of gloom ;
And he shrinks not, from their chill addressing,
    Then, like one who stumbles o'er a tomb.

" Time is short." Glad sound for heart that
        grieveth ;
    Brief the space, ere tears of earth will dry !
" 'Tis the Will of God :" so Faith achieveth
    Noblest deeds, beneath His chastening eye.

19

SPRING VIOLETS.

THRICE welcome, gentle strangers !   Say,
  What tokens do ye bring,
From southern realms where flowers are gay,
  Sweet violets of Spring ?

Queen Summer's heralds ! have ye sped,
  Before her path of bloom,
A broidered mantle to outspread,
  And give her feet soft room ?

Or do your purple buds have birth,
  Ere the tyrant Storm-breath goes,
To braid Hope's tri-color for Earth,
  With snow-drop and primrose ?

Or are your tearful blossoms bent,
  With such a weight of dew,
For human dreams of gladness, meant
  To fall and fade like you ?

Or come you not, to tell us how,
  A meek and lowly mind,
Though far above it wild winds sough,
  True blessedness may find.

In every spot where God says, " Live !"
  Such mind from dusty ways
And from untrodden paths, may give
  Its quiet voice of praise ?

Oh ! could we but reflect, like you,
  Our Father's loving smile—
On sun-bright lawn to Him be true,
  And true in dark defile—

Vain were the wish to mount on high
   With eagle's tireless wing ;
For Heaven within our hearts would lie—
   Sweet violets of Spring !

DEAL GENTLY WITH THY SERVANT, LORD !

Gently, ah ! gently, Lord ! for Thou art
    strong—
  Strong with Infinitude—and I am frail ;
        O let my want avail !
Deal with me gently ! leave me not among
  Sin's wild weird shadows, of my soul ab-
    horred—
        Gently, ah gently, Lord !

And yet I ask not joy should be allowed
  To build rare sun-bows o'er my saddened
    head,
        From tears I long have shed :
19*

Sunlight would dazzle one so used to cloud
  And sea-spray. Give but footing while I ford!
        Gently, ah gently, Lord !

Life hath no pain, Thy presence will not cheer:
  But Thy felt presence fades too oft in pain ;
          And pale hands feebly strain
To clasp thy robe, when only cloud seems
    near—
  Thy cloud of judgment, cold as death-fraught
    sword—
        Gently, ah gently, Lord !

For in Thy frown is horror. Fiends withdraw
  When Thou art smiling; but with endless file
          Close in when fades Thy smile.
Oh Shield of Israel ! let Thy kindness awe
  My soul from sinning ; hear my sighs long-
    poured—
        Gently, ah gently, Lord !

I plead, as one enthralled in labyrinth,
 Who with numb fingers scarce can hold the clue;
   Whose bleeding feet oft rue
The unseen pitfall, or the jaggéd plinth :—
 Take Thou my hand, and in it keep Faith's
  cord—
    Gently, ah gently, Lord !

I know Thy ways are right, but I am blind,
 And faint with year-long groping. One sure
  touch
   Of Thine, would heal so much
Of doubt and sorrow, which no balsam find
 Save of Thy blending. Then relief afford—
    Gently, ah gently, Lord !

Send Peace or Patience ! Patience to believe,
 Though Peace be hidden, till Death's opening
  hinge
   Bid her clear rose-lamp tinge

The Bridegroom's vesture; while glad angels
weave
Crowns for the comers to His festal board—
Gently, ah gently, Lord !

THE LONELY CHRISTMAS.

I DWELL apart, with agéd heart,
  Though blithe young forms about me
Trace out no plan on Pleasure's chart,
  They deem complete without me.
And this is well. In lonely shell
  Why seek love's pearl to smother?
When through this world its gleam may tell
  Love's brilliance in Another?

Among the rest, with smile and jest,
  I mingle, differing only
In silent thoughts of some who blest
  My life, but left me lonely.
Their loss, through years of longing tears, '
  Mine upward vision blinded;

I looked on graves, and shrouds, and biers—
    So now I am not minded.

Ah, no ! through each fast-widening breach
    In home-ranks Time disbandeth,
I view a white-robed army reach
    The Throne-Room where HE standeth ;
Whose Infant-Breath thro' world of death
    Sent Life's glad current bounding ;
Whose Love-in-Death to mourners saith,
    " All grief My love is rounding !"

And festal glee, once sad to me,
    This Faith in Him can hallow ;
While hung in Christmas boughs I see
    A nest of Hopes yet callow—
That chirp and sing, ere long to spring
    And waft, on full-grown pinion,
My lonely soul, where Love's true King
    Hath opulent dominion.

SHADOWS AND SUNSHINE.

Out of the Sunlight, into the shade,
Move without murmuring, unaffrayed !
    He, who leads thee thither,
    Knows what flowers would wither
Earliest underneath the ray,
Of intensely glorious day.
    Not from ridges hilly
    Riseth Hope's white lily;
Glades where runnels wind and turn
Oftenest shelter Faith's low fern ;
And Love's moss hath greener tint
Where the Day-beams rarely glint.

Then, since gentle Christian graces
Burgeon best in shadowy places;
Grieve not, if thy course be laid
Out of the sunlight—into the shade.

Out of the Shadow—into the Sun!
Changes the call, when once growth is won!
   And no fear, lest blossoms wither,
   Clouds the angels' hest "Come hither."
Faith and Hope and Love blaze soon
All unharmed in Heaven's broad noon,
   God's own glory blending.
   There, His grace unending
Streams, in radiance soft as dew,
On souls that tribulation knew;
These, in cave and dungeon's night,
Struggled, ere they soared to light—
Yet a little space, and thou,
Shivering in the gloaming now,

Wilt behold their martyr-faces,

Share their peace in heavenly places,

And pass forever—with Christ made one—

Out of the Shadow—into the Sun !

20

IN THE CITY OF REFUGE.

THE blood of souls is on my hand—
　　A stain no grief will clear away ;
My days from peace are rightly bann'd,
　　Since, traveling on the world's highway,
Each smouldering fire I left unfann'd,
　　Each reed unlifted, where it lay.

I can recall unholy deeds
　　And wayward musings—offerings lame—
The look that shunn'd a brother's needs—
　　Love of man's praising—fear of blame—
And careless words, like poison-weeds
　　Stifling the wishes Faith might frame.

But as an ocean-column rears
   Its crest of gloom, and seamen scares,
With sullen frown and murmurs fierce,
   Thus o'er me, darkening dreams and prayers,
Hangs in a cloud I cannot pierce,
   Mine evil done at unawares.

Safe though my own poor life may be,
   Enwalled in bulwarks sure and strong ;
Thence baffled though the avenger flee,
   Yet thoughts of grief must rankle long,
While in his grasp of doom I see
   Friends left unwarned of woe and wrong.

Ah blesséd lives ! whence float afar
   The seeds of blessing, heaven-diffused—
No futilé pangs your memories scar, .
   For time and treasure, loans unused ;
Foreshadowing now the Final Bar,
   And sounds of wailing, self-accused.

High-Priest and Judge, Thy dying breath
   Plead for unconscious guilt.   Oh see,
How souls I warned not, throng to death :
   Dear Lord, thy power can make them flee,
While yet the Avenger lingereth,
   Back to their Refuge-home—to Thee !

ANOTHER GRIEF.

Against my heart as with a gauntlet knocking,
    Another Grief is here:
I know the sound, and spring with eager locking
    To keep my threshold clear;
But Grief *will* enter, wild refusal mocking
    And barrier-arm of fear.

Oh were my heart an Inn, where like a Palmer
    Grief some short hours would stay,
With Eastern odors prove a Thought-embalmer,
    And reckoning more than pay,
Through one sweet grain to hold me purer,
        calmer,
    Left, when it passed away;

I could come forth, with loyal gaze beholding
    Tokens each new Grief brings ;
Take from Love's last bright lamp the silver
        moulding,
    Claimed for the King of Kings ;
And yet believe the robe of serge enfolding
    An angel's radiant wings.

But now as in a vault 'neath gray church-altar,
    My burried Sorrows lie ;
While I have learned to join in hymn and psalter,
    As though no tombs were nigh ;
To pace the aisles with feet that rarely falter,
    And passive, tearless eye.

How can I bear another Grief to marsha
    Down to that place of fears ?—
Where Griefs not dead, but lulled in stillness
        partial,
    (The death-like swoon of years

Dispelled at once by torch-gleam shining far)
    shall
  Move on their quiet biers—

Move on their biers, and rising, throng around
    me,
  Each half-forgotten ghost,
Pale with the thorn-band whereof Time dis-
    crowned me,
  Asking, in silent boast,
" Art thou come down to loosen chains that
    bound me
  Among this vanquished host ?"

Oh, faithless dreamer ! not with message cruel,
  But, breathing tenderness,
Comes every Grief to thee,—God's signet jewel
  Each wore, its work to bless—
Nor, though with anguish seems thy life a duel,
  Wish thou one courier less !

For all were needed, all some due monition
 To thee in love address'd ;
And then, rejoicing in their closéd mission,
 Lay, white-robed, down to rest,
As martyr souls, in Apostolic vision,
 Await their Lord's behest.

And thou at last, the long sad lessoning ended,
 Thy Vault of Griefs wilt see
Changed to a Court, by shining ranks defended :
 And their All-Hail shall be
The angelic Gloria in Excelsis, blended
 With peace—good-will to thee !

OUR BROKEN VINE.

THROUGH years of growth we twined, with
    gentlest care,
        All tendrils fair—
Marking their promise, may-fly plucked, and
    worm
        From leaf and germ—
And planted, where east wind were earliest felt
        A close larch-belt.

Our thoughts went onward till, with Time's
    advance,
        Green leaves should dance
O'er our south lattice, and sun-checkered flow
        Of vine-shade throw—

Well was it for our peace we could not see
    Things soon to be !

For in the night-time near our vine's light frame,
    Despoilers came,
And low in dust the shielding arbor laid
    Our toil had made :
From sleep secure we rose, to grieve at morn
    O'er life-veins torn ;—

To strive in vain from ruin to uplift,
    With anxious thrift ;
And a soft purple bloom anew to gain
    For clusters slain.
Not for our old age now will strong boughs
    shoot
    Their wealth of fruit.

Foiled in our plannings, shall we spend in tears
    These blightful years ?

Nay ! One yet lives whose skill decay can stop,
    With deathless prop,
And through the enclosure where our vine lies
    low,
        His step we know.

Oh Hand of Love ! once wounded, lift and
    prune
        Our treasure soon !
And from dark midnight foes, in wait to steal,
        The saved fruit seal !
To Thee ! O Heart of Pity ! we resign
        Our broken Vine !

UNCLOTHED.

YIELD up now the kingly purple, long the
    birthright of thy pride—
View the eyes that sought thy greeting, coldly
    droop or turn aside—
Let the presence, once so regal, lose the rose-
    lined cloak of Wealth—
From the slender form it shielded, lift the fair
    white tunic, Health.

Next unwind the broidered girdle, long en-
    circling heart and frame,
With the genial warmth of Friendship—with
    the royal zone—Good Name ;

Then unfasten clasp and armlet, and strip off
    yet costlier things :
From thy head· Hope's crown of beauty, from
    thy hand Love's golden rings.

Yet more penury thou needest : from thy spirit
    take the cheer,
That, with shield of Faith, undaunted faced
    the armaments of Fear ;
Till from eye fades look of calmness, till from
    lip fades smile of trust—
While thy friends have home and pleasaunce,
    let thy place be low in dust. .

But remember all thus taken was thy willing-
    hearted gift,
When before thy Saviour kneeling, thou in
    Love's first glad unthrift,

21

Saidst, " Dear Lord, I can but offer all I have
    or hope to be;
Give the worldling this world's treasure—craves
    my spirit none but Thee !"

And each joy unclaimed while left thee, hung
    on tenure of His will :
Hath the glow of first love faded ?—pledge
    and promise bind thee still.
Darest thou mourn that robes and relics of old
    idols strew the sod ?
Darest thou murmur through thy mourning—
    " I have nothing left but God ?"

CLOTHED UPON.

WHEN the cross, assumed, it may be, lightly,
  On weak nature leans with galling weight ;
When thy heart-sins, grieved for once but
       slightly,
  Rise dilating, shrouding e'en Heaven's
      gate ;

Desert-days recall ! Thy Lord was tempted,
  Left a target for the Fiend alone,
Left till all weird stores of malice emptied—
  Pomp and pageant with their Prince had
      flown.

Rarely yet, while circled jest and laughter,
    Felt one heart the influence angels* bring :
Silence first must fall.   That silence after,
    Comes caress of peace from radiant wing.

If rough hand of Pain fair limnings cancel,
    From thy Hall of Life, once fresco-bright,
Let the broad blank space enclose a chancel ;
    Holy laws of Love around it write.

Seems thy nature worthless, dark, unable
    For man's good—God's glory—aught to plan?
There, as on a background densely sable,
    Grace in full effulgence, all may scan.

Think, though bungler palette needs, and pencils
    Fashioned, ere he paint, by faultless rule ;
Shapes false contours oft with fine utensils,
    And for fault and failure blames his tool—

* There is a German superstition that when a circle of friends become silent, an angel is passing among them, and the one who first breaks silence, has been touched by the angel's wing.

Yet a charred wand, near true Artist lying,
  In his grasp all deft an outline draws,
Where, forms of truth at once descrying,
  Untaught eye must give its prompt applause.

'Tis thy Master's hand each color chooses—
  Though as yet no gold or crimson glow
In thy life, with darker shade, He fuses—
  Thou his full designing canst not know.

Rude the sketch may seem, yet if, when finished
  Smirch and flaw in soft haze disappear ;
If by test of Heaven's blaze undiminished
  Lights scarce noted gleam from centres clear,

Thou wilt own how things whose touch abases,
  Though like charcoal dust, of man flung by,
May God's power, in long undreamed of phases,
  As with diamond splendor glorify.

21*

A GARDEN THOUGHT.

WITH fence of blossom, leaf and briar,
 The Summer folds from view
Yon gleaming river, belfry spire,
 And half the hill-range blue,
Yielding of late, from dawn to night,
My winter-wearied gaze delight.

Yet soft the shade in leafy niche,
 And lovingly a scent
From briar and blossom comes to witch
 With fragrance, till, content,
I peer not through my woodland screen
To note the haze on heights serene.

And if, from landscape of my life
    The wintry look might go—
If lawn and leaf, with sweetness rife,
    Replaced the year-long snow—
Then, doubtless, were more rarely conn'd
Far splendors of the Hills beyond.

ROUND HILL, MASS.

HAVELOCK AT ALUMBAGH.

Soldier ! along whose tropic way
    Of sun-glare, lay
Prayers, strewn like blossoms for decay—
No lonely leaf or petal lost,
Hereafter those now trampled most,
    In depth of Hindoo mould,
Will more luxuriant buds unfold
    To grace the gladsome day,
When Earth's dark tribes, no longer far astray,
To Him of many crowns salaam of heart shall
    pay.

Slowly the sea-winds waft along
    Praise warm and strong :

But pale he lies, to whom belong
A nation's thanks, though round him swell
Echoes from home-launched caravel.
  Ah, tardy-winged ! one day
Of hastier flight through storm and spray,
  And the brave heart had known
How England's heart throbbed fast from hut
  to throne,
With love and pride and sorrow, henceforth all
  his own.

O'er tent and tower falls noontide glare
  Of Indian air ;
But on one calm brow sheltered there
Never shall sunbeams smite again—
Foot-march or toil of battle pain.
  For the field-weary head
There is a safe pavilion spread :
  Prayers for his dear life, o'er

Its threshold-faltering, found him passed be-
      fore,
Found, too, their own true meaning—life for
      evermore !

    Nor on thy last puissant deed—
        Babes, mothers, freed,
   While Moslem shapes and swords recede,
   Alone with deepening love we think—
   But rather with thy life-work link
       Faith, that in sleep-snatched hour
  Won at the Cross its shield of power—
      Pagoda, whence the strain
Of prayer went up, that not one idol-fane
With spot of shade might fleck the Sun of
      Christ's broad reign.

    Long sank thy fame, like cereus-bloom
        In bed of gloom,
   Its fibres for one hour's perfume :

Then with rich fragrance filled Earth's room,
And lingers deathless round thy tomb.
    From the unobtrusive root
Only at midnight flowers might shoot,.
    And careless eyes now weep
Because thro' years imperill'd, dim with sleep
O'er plant so precious, they no watch of love
        could keep.

Yet, as in ancient Spanish scene,
    Love crowned the queen
Whose sweet life ebbed, her rank unseen,—
Thus, Warrior! Christian hearts endow
Thy memory, though among us thou
    Wilt never move, to hear
High magnates' greeting, people's cheer,
    Nor voices, dearer far,
Whose silence could even Rhineland's beauty
        mar;
That rose o'er war's wild clash, as o'er cloud-
        seas some star.

Thy loyal heart, with odorous gum
 Of fame, would come
To Jesus' feet, and hush the hum
Of earthly-praise.   To Him we leave
Thy bliss—our anthem's loudest breve
 Lost in His word, " Well done !"
Unheeded, in His joy begun.
 Tried Ruler, henceforth dwell
Not in a treason-haunted citadel—
Rule thou o'er ransomed tribes of realms where
 none rebel !

RIVER BURIAL.

THEY buried their Chief in the river,
   Watching the dark wave close
O'er sins of its first fame-giver—
   Over his long-borne woes.

Oft, on my own strength squandered,
   Tracing out pathways drear,
I muse, as De Soto pondered
   On red foes ambushed near;

Till weary and faint with the fever,
   Breathed in from a swamp-like world,
With search for Earth's golden lever,
   Through tangles where snakes lie curled;

Back to my couch of repenting,
   Friends of old years I call ;
Hope ! Love ! hear my heart's relenting—
   Faith ! Courage ! how needed all !

Under this midnight of sorrow,
   Lit by Heaven's starlight clear,
Your hands must a grave-place borrow,
   And straighten my Past on its bier.

Visions of joy from Youth's quiver
   Hasting o'er valley and hill,
Bury ye low in the River,
   Of God my Redeemer's Will !

Fears 'neath whose mist diurnal,
   Ever my chilled thoughts cower,
Calm be their sleep, and eternal,
   In the broad flood of His Power !

Lower than these shall be buried
   Self, while in trance it lies—
Lest its longings, a phalanx serried,
   Wake up, with revengeful cries.

So perish all foes that grimly
   Pillow of frail heart haunt !
They are gone—yet that heart still dimly
   Quails, conscious of deeper want ;

Till the Saviour, strong to deliver,
   Bending her couch above,
Shall bury her sins in a river—
   The River of God's free Love !

ICONOCLASM.

Through the fair Cathedral of thy Home
   Have Idol-breakers rushed ?
Lie saint, and jeweled shrine, and dome,
   In one dark ruin crushed ?
Did Sorrows, in malignant swarm,
At once from gate to belfry storm,
And hast thou stood appalled to hear their hum,
While waiting for the worst, thyself a statue
    dumb ?

In dreary silence, dost thou gaze
   On wreck of all things dear,
Feeling familiar notes of praise
   Grate harshly on thine ear !

Doubting if ever through the fane

Can incense-bearers stream again ;

Or pleasant pictures, bright with human love,

Bear, on assumption-clouds, thy soul toward

    heaven above ?

Slight are the causes, frail, unfeared,

    That desolation bring ;

Shrines through a life-time's toil upreared

    One day may downward fling :

And still the shell of home be there,

The void within—how bleak and bare !

When nooks, wherein of old we knelt to pray,

Are lost for ever—dashed in one brief hour

    away.

And yet, if Christ's forgotten Word,

    Though while from missal sung

It trembled on the air unheard,

    Now teach in household tongue :

If shattered idols yield their place
To Him, whose meek unpictured Face
Smiles on us ever—will we but invoke
His aid, His presence—then how needful each
    rough stroke !

'Tis through His will the homes we love
   Are rifled, lest they hold
Some chapel toward whose fair alcove
   Thoughts turn, as sheep to fold.
There is a safer, holier fane !
Its glory no assault may stain,
Why stand we gazing here on vacant niche,
When angels show the Home, beyond imagin-
    ing rich ?

NEVER PRAY FOR TRIALS.

Blooms thy life like a vale-born lily,
 Shielded from storms by coppice shade ?
Crave not the coming of Frost-breath chilly
 To show thee strong although Summer fade,
   Nor sigh for change !

Nor sigh for change !   In gladness bask—
To smile and bud thy joyful task.
It is not hard while days are bright
 To know and feel the Sunbeams near ;
But Faith, till now unfaltering, might
 Bend with the blast, were darkness here.

Should gardener's hand that coppice hew,
 And give wild winds of trial room,
Thy dying roots might long for dew,
 Thy leaves for roof of cedarn gloom,
And white bells wilting, calyx torn,
The peace once undervalued mourn.

Soars hope of thine on dove-like pinion ?
 And sings thy heart in carol sweet ?
Call not that heart an idle minion
 For whom rough hours of pain were meet,
   Nor sigh for change !

For change is coming.   Long and dark
Thy galley toil may prove.   Some mark
Of anguish like our Lord's, must lie
 On each wan forehead, would we gain
His City's freedom, ere we die.
 And if as yet no touch of pain

Have marred thy visage, let him choose
  What hour He pleases, to imprint
The signing none He loves may lose—
  The seal unworn by face of flint !
Pray not for trials ! meekly range
Through mercies left—nor sigh for change !

THE STARLESS CROWN.

She lay upon a dying bed,
  And down her cheeks sad tears were flowing—
Not in lament for youthful head
  Beneath the turf so early going.
The maiden knew, from Jesus' love
  No mound of earth her soul might sever ;
And in His presence longed to prove
  Fulness of peace forever.

Yet on that orb-like joy arose
  One gloom-spot half the radiance marring :
No rescued soul from rank of foes
  Won for her Lord, her crown was starring.

She had not toiled, like some who flee,
  To use brief space ere curfew's tolling;
And o'er her mind a billowy sea
  Of late remorse came rolling.

Grief-laden tale ! through heart of mine
  The dead girl's shivered lance now bearing
To rouse the thought—When souls resign
  Their worn-out mail, for home preparing,
Shall I through Pearly Gate *alone*
  Pass to my rest, no saved one leading ;
While angels marvel, " Are there none
  Lost through her lukewarm pleading ?"

I cannot tell.   A wayside word
  From happier lips, may fall supinely .
In good soil, to spring unheard,
  And bloom at length in bliss divinely ;
While costly cedars oft will droop
  In sunniest nook of pleasaunce planted,

And die, though cares around them group,
 And prayer each-root hath haunted.

Still, from my being's depth there cries
 One wish, o'er all dear wishes reigning—
(Like fibrous gold that underlies
 All earth-clods with its own clear veining)
To form my Lord but one fair shaft,
 And leave it in His saintly quiver,
Then pass away, as broken haft
 Sinks down in silent river.

Once sated with that glorious spoil—
 That seen reward thus crowning labor,
Outweighing all Life's battle-toil,
 Or anguish keen as thrust of sabre—
A SOUL REDEEMED! Complaint must die,
 Though ills like thorns on cactus thicken;
In dull heart's core no joy could lie,
 That whisper would not quicken.

Wait—wait—too eager Will ! and learn
  O'er seed when sown 'tis vain to hover,
And, with a child's impatience, turn
  The loam of young blade's darksome cover.
Be thou content, if every eve
  Some work of Love, thy faith adorning,
Lie buried with the Sun, and leave
  Glad issues until Morning !

23

ANCHORED, YET WEARY.

Acts xxvii. 29.

ANCHORED, yet weary, and wishing for day,
For a glimpse of the harbor where home-ban-
    ners play,
For the brightness lining Death's solemn cloud,
And for faith to enter, by fear unbowed.

Were youth's islets sunny, long left behind ?
Ah ! tears well fast while we call to mind
How dazzling the ripples that near them lay—
We are anchored, yet weary, and wishing for
    day.

Yet fairer the sunlight that lies before,

On the cloud-veiled Hills our Redeemed ex-
plore :

But ere timbrels can triumph, hang storm-
winds and spray

Round the anchored, yet weary, and wishing
for day.

Would yon Hills seem fair, but for tempest's
frown?

With the Cross uplifted, who hails the Crown?

Not in smooth seas will the mariner stay

Anchored, yet weary, and wishing for day.

Like the saint on whose eyelash hung ever a tear,

Though his smile was radiant with glory near ;

Heaven's joy and Earth's gloom interlacing
alway,

Leave us anchored, yet weary, and wishing for
day.

PRAYER OF ONE NO LONGER
PRAYED FOR.

PRAYERS poured forth in saintly alms,
　　Once this feeling heart made stronger;
Gave my dead joys burial-balms:
　　Now they soothe no longer.

Lips on whose dear prayers we lean,
　　Press in turn the chalice, Sorrow:
Friends who wept our woes yestreen,
　　Weep their own to-morrow.

Quickly though that cup pass on,
　　Tarrieth long the wormwood essence;
Gay hearts deem its memory gone
　　Ere one gall-taste lessens.

In the earlier hours of woe,
    All who loved me shared my grieving—
Prayers, with tears in precious flow,
    Half my loss retrieving ;

While my fainting soul they bore
    Near to Heaven on wings of praying,
Made her feel, through crystal door,
    Warmth and splendors straying.

Sweet, while undissolved her swoon,
    There to lie, quiescent, lowly !
Came the awakening all too soon ;—
    Earthward sinking slowly,

Sounds of tumult broke with jar
    Roughly on my balméd musing—
Prayerful echoes died afar,
    Mine in new grief losing.

Then the storms of Earth rushed in,
    Whirled and howled from hearth to case-
        ment—
Fiery cords of discipline
    Lashed to self-abasement.

Now for interceding word,
    That like Heaven-born air refreshes,
Pants my soul, as pants a bird
    Beating wiry meshes.

If but one true heart alone
    Sought the solace I am needing,
Soon were hope and succor won
    Pledged to that fond pleading.

One true heart ?   Ah weary breast !
    Crave no draught from goblet earthen ;
He whose glance can grief arrest
    Views thy veiléd burthen.

Champion who, in legends hoar,
    Gazed on Holy Cup of Sorrow,
Through his after-quest forbore
    Help of man to borrow.

If for thee the San Grail shine,
    Drink ! the touch of Christ remaineth :
He shall find its bitter wine
    Sweet, with Christ who reigneth.

COUNT LOUIS OF NASSAU.

"Count Louis, finding that the day was lost, and his army all cut to pieces, rallied around him a little band of troopers, among whom were his brother Count Henry, and Duke Christopher, son of the Elector Palatine, and together they made a final and desperate charge. It was the last that was ever seen of them on earth. They all went down together in the midst of the fight, and were never heard of more.

"It is difficult to find in history a more frank and loyal character. All who knew him loved him........ His mother always addressed him as her dearly beloved, her heart's cherished Louis. 'You must come soon to me,' she wrote in the last year of his life, 'for I have many matters to ask your advice upon, and I thank you beforehand that you have loved me as your mother all the days of your life, for which may God Almighty have you in His holy keeping.'

"The Prince of Orange, meanwhile passed days of intense anxiety, expecting hourly to hear from his brothers, listening to dark rumors which he refused to credit, and could not contradict, and writing letters day after day, long after the eyes which should have read the friendly missives were closed." RISE OF THE DUTCH REPUBLIC.

ANOTHER night is near,

Yet home they come not. Must the Rachael-cry

Of heart-pang, hastening down from earliest

year,

Find sad renewal over pall and bier

Where patriot heroes lie?

Fields have been lost before.
Let but one precious life be safe as then,
And free hearts will not grudge their jeweled
    store,
Nor free hands fail their Chief's fresh path to bore
    Through Alva's close-ranked men.

Between him and the foe
Some river doubtless runs, as ran erewhile
The Ems' bright wave. His mother soon shall
    know
That frank, kind voice, more dear than music's
    flow—
    Soon hail her darling's smile.

A thousand perils pass'd—
And all look shallow—then, too oft we find
Their depth unfathomed. She has looked her last
On those clear eyes—on hands that wove so fast
    Thought threads of warrior mind.

The Silent Prince hath seen
All summer friends from tryst and council fade ;
While brothers' love and truth still rose, be-
    tween
His heart and the cold world, an evergreen
    Of belting winter shade.

    But Love can never lay
Those forms so cherished in cathedral crypt,
Nor press long kisses on beloved clay—
That clay to dust will moulder, far away
    By band of spoilers stripp'd.

    Not safer did they lie
Where old Crusaders planted Syrian sward !*
All fields are holy where believers die—
Cross-overshadowed, sunned by wakeful Eye
    Of Death's triumphant Lord.

* The Campo Santo of Pisa, was covered with earth brought from Palestine by the earlier crusaders.

Though angels have not borne
Those dear ones home, as once from Sinai's
steep,
They a dead pilgrim to the Rhine ere morn
Bare, that fond sister's touches might adorn
And sister-voices weep :

Yet to an Altar-Home
The Spirits of our Martyrs have been led ;
With palm and robe invested, washed from
loam
Of worldly strife, and 'neath celestial Dome
Wait, with the kingly Dead,

For all who pass away
While scourge and smoke-wreath twist their
chariot line ;
For all whose heart-scourge, falling but to flay,
Gives through a long life scarce one holiday—
Poor mother ! such was thine !

I WILL GIVE HIM THE MORNING STAR.

Rev., chap. ii., v. 28.

———•———

" Where may happier lot be seen
  Than hath crowned my soul's fair queen ?
  Flowers spring up where'er she strayeth—
  Only sunshine round her playeth ;
  Yet the flowers and sunshine free,
  Look not half so bright as she.

" Late, she raised her dreaming eye
  To a sister-star on high ;
  And I prayed, with murmur low,
  ' Ah, my own love, gaze not so !
  Glorious though yon star may be,
  For I cannot give it thee.' "

Thus, oppressed by mournful sense
Of his proud heart's impotence,
Once, an earthly lover, sighing,
Weighed the love he deemed undying,
Found it infinite in will—
Feeble to avert one ill.

Well may higher Love rejoice
In the Heavenly Bridegroom's voice ;
He, a universe surveying,
Far-off worlds His sign obeying,
Saith to all who faithful are—
" I will give the Morning-Star !"

Star of Faith ! serene and strong,
Comrade of that Angel song,
Whose rich harmony, descending
O'er meek swains their folds defending,
Silence filled with joy, and night
With a rush of argent light ;—

24

Lead us, as thou ledd'st of yore,
Magian from his midnight lore—
From the Crucible of Thought,
Where he long solution sought
Of Life's problems, dark and lorn—
To the Babe in Beth-le-hem born!

Star of Christ! unvalued gift!
Gleaming down the abysmal rift
Where the world's vain pomp and clamor
Chain us with resistless glamor;
Win our love from fame and pelf—
From the veiled idol—Self!

Cease not o'er these hearts to throw
Radiant leash, Love's path to show,
Till their frail and fleshly awning
Rend, and thus reveal the dawning
Of a Day no night can mar—
Heralded by Morning-Star!

BY THE BRINK OF THE RIVER.

THEY laid me by the River's brink
　　Long, very long ago,
And " Jesus will not let you sink,
　　Be fearless"—whispered low.

So near me drew the Pilot, Death,
　　So close the waters came,
It seemed on each ice-laden breath
　　Hung heavily my name.

And once—it was a wondrous view—
　　My pain-worn eyes espied
A magnet star-wreath, strong to woo
　　The soul to yonder side.

But years went by, and still unheard
  The call we deemed so near,
And still, thro' secret sign deterred,
  The Pilot left me here.

Left me, yet in the busy field
  Of toil, where God is served,
Not to go forth again, and wield
  The sickle whence I swerved.

Left me, in silence and alone,
  To muse and marvel, why
So many in their bloom have gone
  While I unsummoned lie.

Kind faces that my wan mouth kiss'd,
  And prayed " God speed her, home !"
Have blended with the River's mist,
  Like sun-bows with sea-foam.

It may be, holier hearts would watch
 Till through yon cloud-veil dim
Turrets of gold shone out, and catch
 The songs of Seraphim.

For this my faith is far too weak,
 My spirit-wings are soiled ;
They cannot cleave the mist, and seek
 The Light within it coiled.

Nor dare I from the water's edge
 Bright thoughts, like lilies glean ;
Too swift thy roll, too rank thy sedge,
 O stream of the Unseen !

Yet, like the chiming of far bells
 That chime from viewless shore,
Sometimes a waft of music swells
 Above the waves' uproar.

-24*

That sound, though seldom heard, hath
dulled
The stirring tunes of Earth,
And made her songs, once foldly culled,
Seem now of slender worth.

Thus, for the mandate of my Prince,
I look and linger still ;
Useless, and yet unmurmuring, since
I know it is His Will.

L'ENVOI.

WHILE softly upon Earth's chill breast
  The quiet snow-flakes pour,
Her look, beneath that hueless vest,
  Grows drearier than before ;
Yet the fast-showering crystals wrap
With love the riches of her lap :

And when long hours of sunlight come
  Shall turf and woodland pay
With lavish blossoms—bees' glad hum—
  For Winter's white array,
That fostered, in its mantle warm
All charms of fragrance, hue and form.

And thus, if words of holy cheer
    On mourning spirits lie
With lifeless weight, while home looks drear,
    And Heaven no longer nigh—
Covering, as with a cold white mask,
Thoughts that for vanished love-warmth ask.

Yet through their force, the winter fled,
    Fresh buds of joy and trust,
And vivid green of praise, may spread
    Above that snow-bound crust;
For Christ to weariest heart can bring
Treasures of sunlight, love and Spring.